Shotgun Granny
 & Jesus

PALMETTO
PUBLISHING
Charleston, SC
www.PalmettoPublishing.com

Copyright © 2024 by Dr. Al Shifflett

All rights reserved

No portion of this book may be reproduced, stored in a retrieval system, or transmitted in any form by any means–electronic, mechanical, photocopy, recording, or other–except for brief quotations in printed reviews, without prior permission of the author.

Paperback ISBN: 979-8-822962-52-1

Shotgun Granny & Jesus

AND OTHER SHORT STORIES

DR. AL SHIFFLETT

I dedicate this book to my two grandsons,
Noah, who lives in Bluffton, SC, and Nathan,
serving in the Coast Guard in Sitka,
Alaska with his wife Ali, and two boys,
Mayson and Matthew.

Contents

Chapter One: Shotgun Granny & Jesus   1

Chapter Two: The Motivator   9

Chapter Three: The Red-letter Jesus Bible   35

Chapter Four: Blue Ice Patrol   42

Chapter Five: Out of Egypt   59

Chapter Six: The Tree of Life   70

Chapter Seven: Finders Keepers. Losers Weepers   77

About the Author   90

Chapter One

Shotgun Granny & Jesus

My 96 year-old Grandmother, Jeanetta Cooper, lived on three acres next to the chocolate factory. She'd strapped on the side of her motorized chair a canister of hot pepper spray and a 380 raspberry Ruger pistol, and a shotgun on her lap which was given to her by her Uncle Harry. She had a sign plastered on the back of the chair that read, *Semper Paratus*, which was Latin for *"always ready,"* the moto of the Coast Guard. Her grandson Nathan was in the Coast Guard and that's how she learned about the motto. It suited her well as thirty years ago, she was assaulted by two teenagers who'd knocked her to the ground, snatched her purse, and left her with a broken hip. Physically, she never fully recovered from the broken hip. Mentally she was sharp as a tack, and upon leaving the rehab center she vowed "never again," and that she'd be *Semper Paratus!*

CHAPTER ONE

The day she left the rehab center she went straight to Wal-Mart and bought the canister of hot pepper spray. Next stop was the local gun shop which offered free firing lessons and a Concealed Weapons Permit for anyone who bought a gun over three-hundred bucks. Granny's 380 raspberry Ruger cost three-hundred twenty-five. She took the class and got her CWP. She was loaded for bear, meanwhile, her Uncle Harry, unaware of the Ruger purchase, gave her the shotgun.

Although confined to the motorized chair she became proficient as a shooter, winning awards in her age category. Of course, in her age category no one was shooting against her! They were all dead. With the pistol, Granny hit Bulls-eye eight out of ten times, and blew the target away with the shotgun! But Granny was different; and darn good! She wasn't called *Shotgun Granny* for nothing.

She lived alone with her two cats, Bonnie and Clyde, along with Jesus, a hundred twenty-five-pound Rottweiler. Clyde was grey with white markings except for a black spot around one eye; like someone slugged him. Clyde was a rascal cat always getting into trouble. He turned the light switches on and off and flushed the bathroom commode whenever the bathroom door was left open. The water bill went sky high until Granny figured out what Clyde was doing. Bonnie, a big yellow cat was no trouble at all, just slept and ate and followed Clyde around. It appeared that even in the cat world good women were attracted to bad men.

Granny already had Bonnie and Clyde when Jesus was a second coming. The day Jesus came there was no trumpet blowing, he just sorta' fell out of the sky, like manna from heaven. He showed up one day in Granny's front yard half starved to death. Granny fed and watered him and after posting his picture around town no one claimed him. *Finders keepers losers weepers.* The dog was nameless until that fateful day when she rode out to the mailbox at the end of the lane to get her mail. As fate would have it; an illegal alien came out of the bushes, slipped up behind Granny, and put a knife to her throat. Big mistake!

The nameless Rottweiler watching Granny from the front porch saw what was happening, raced down the sidewalk like one of Samson's foxes with his tail on fire, and leaped on the back of that illegal alien shaking him like a skunk. The skunk peed in his pants and was last seen running down the street with blood streaming down the back of his shirt screaming and snorting cuss words like the demonic hogs that drowned in the Sea of Galilee. The Rottweiler had saved Granny's life and earned his honorable name—Jesus!

And oh, Jesus and Bonnie and Clyde got along like peaches and cream, like love and marriage, like a horse and carriage. After that, anywhere that Granny went, Jesus went. She was well taken care of, as Jesus was her bodyguard watching out for her. After all, who's gonna' mess with a 96-year-old crazed Shotgun Granny and a hundred-twenty-five pound Rottweiler named Jesus? Not me, and I'm just one of her grandsons.

+ + +

Hazelton, was a small South Carolina town just off I-95 with three exits and a population of about seven thousand residents. Hazelton however, was unlike a lot of dying Lowcountry towns; Hazelton was thriving and growing. Hazelton had three things going for it—a seminary, a chocolate factory, and finally, a wheelchair factory. The Hazelton Evangelical Seminary was the largest seminary east of the Mississippi River, with over five-hundred students counting the on-line registrations, and HCF—the Hazelton Chocolate Factory employed over seven

CHAPTER ONE

hundred people. The Hazelton Motorized Chair Factory, known simply as HMC actually put Hazelton on the map as they employed over two-thousand people and made the best motorized wheelchairs this side of China. Granny's chair, of course, was the finest chair HMC made. It cost upward to fifty thousand dollars and was equal to the one Stephen Hawkins used in his bout with ALS. Granny said, "If the smartest man on the planet had a chair like that, she deserved one too." With help from the two South Carolina Senators, she got it for twenty thousand. Granny didn't need the speaking apparatus necessary for a patient with ALS like Stephen Hawkins, but her chair did have a built-in smart phone and computer. Wherever they had Wi-fi she was good to go, along with Jesus at her side. All the local businesses in Hazelton knew Granny, and accepted Jesus like a seeing eye dog. Granny and Jesus were inseparable which should be true of every Christian, spiritually speaking, but is not.

It was two o'clock in the afternoon when Granny asked me to take her to the First National Hazelton Bank to deposit a check and then go to the chocolate outlet store to pick up a box of chocolates. Even though she had direct deposit with her social security checks she had a question about what she called a bogus charge from Motel 6 in Beckley, West Virginia. She wanted it cancelled. "Once that's straightened out, we can get my box of chocolates." That was her plan, she loved chocolates. Meanwhile, the quarantine had shut down everything in America and most businesses in the entire country. It was hard to figure out why the bars stayed open and churches remained shut. Money talks even in a pandemic.

"Granny, are you sure you can go inside, why don't you just call them?"

"I don't want a run-around, or talking to a dumb computer, or someone from India—I want to see a real live person and get it taken off my account. And yes, they let one in at a time due to the pandemic, so you wait in the car, as Jesus and I get it straightened out."

"Okay, but put your mask on, you know you're no spring chicken."

Granny strapped on her bright star-spangled patriot mask and mumbled something indistinguishable under the mask as she strapped the elastic bands over both ears. Jesus cocked his head and watched with curiosity. She insisted that I sit in the car. "I may be old but I'm not feeble," she said—"come on Jesus!"

She rolled up to the bank door with Jesus and rang the doorbell. During the pandemic the sign read, "Ring the doorbell and someone will let you enter." Mrs. Wilson, one of the three assistant managers of the bank came to the door with her Covit-19 mask on. "Mrs. Cooper and Jesus, come in—how are you doing?"

"Fine," Granny answered as she entered with Jesus following. "They turned the corner out of sight and entered Mrs. Wilson's office.

"Mrs. Cooper, what a surprise to see you and Jesus out today, you know at your age you could be vulnerable to this virus."

"Oh, I know that, tell me something I don't know."

"Okay, what can I do for you?"

"A hotel charge of $114 dollars, appeared on my bank statement from Beckley, West Virginia, and you know I haven't been out of the state for years, so I want that taken off my account, pronto;"

"Why we sure will," said Mrs. Wilson. "Do you have any relatives in West Virginia, or someone there who knows your account numbers?"

"Not a soul, Jesus and I have never been to Beckley, and don't plan on going."

"Well, have you been out recently and used your debit card, or purchased something online?"

CHAPTER ONE

"Not on your life," said Granny. "Oh, well, the first of the month I went online and bought some lavender smelling, paper pellets for Bonnie and Clyde."

"And you used your debit card?" said Mrs. Wilson.

"Yes, do you think that's how the thief got my card number?"

"It's highly possible, do not order anything online, unless you see a lock revealing that your point of sale is highly secure, and even then, some have figured, how to hack the numbers."

"So, you can take the charge off my account?"

"Yes, but it will take up to three days before it shows a credit on your account, so be patient, and I will have the bank send you a new card as your card has been compromised. Meanwhile, you will not be able to use the old card—in fact, give it to me, and I'll cut it up."

"When will I get a new card?" Granny asked as she handed over the old card.

"It will take up to seven to ten days," replied Mrs. Wilson.

Granny and Jesus came out of the bank and rolled to the van. I jumped out and put the motorized chair up in the back, along with Jesus. Granny didn't say a word as she removed her mask.

"Chocolate factory next," I said.

"No, let's go home. I'm disgusted, besides, Mrs. Wilson had to cut up my debit card and I don't have any money."

"Granny, if you want some chocolate. I'll buy it for you."

"No, I'm disgusted—some redneck has made me angry. But I suppose he needed some shelter as he checked into a hotel using my debit card."

"Why it's awful nice of you to help out a stranger," I said facetiously.

"Yeah, when you do it for the least of these, you do it for Jesus." Jesus perked his head up once he heard his name mentioned."

"Not you, Jesus, go back to sleep," said Granny.

+ + +

I left Granny that evening around dark not knowing that the next day her picture and Jesus would be on the front page of the Hazelton Times and Fox News. It just goes to show that from one day to the next you never know what's coming. Probably a good thing we don't know. According to the police report it happened around 11:30 at night. Granny had gone to bed and was awakened by the sound of breaking glass. She opened her eyes and tuned over staring straight into a flashlight being held by a masked man, and it wasn't the Lone Ranger.

"Don't scream, lady, or I'll shoot you. Where's your money?"

"I don't have any money, get out of my house."

"I heard you have a safe here in your bedroom somewhere."

"You heard wrong, but I do know one thing…"

"What's that, old woman?"

"From now on, I'm sleeping with my Ruger under my pillow."

The masked man laughed. "What in the world would you do with a gun? You couldn't shoot it, even if you had one."

"I'll show you," said Granny. "I can shoot better than any cowardly scumbag thief like you." She paused as she noticed, unknown to the thief, that Jesus had come to the bedroom door and was eyeing him.

The thief laughed again, "Okay, where is your money?"

"You know," said Granny. "You best back out of here, real slow, because Jesus is watching you; and if you make a sudden move Jesus will be on you worse than chicken pox!"

"Well, aren't you something, old woman. You think I care about Jesus. You hypocrites can go to church all you want, and you can cry

CHAPTER ONE

out, "Jesus save me, Jesus save me," and I'm still going to take your money—and Jesus can't do one darn thing about it."

Granny leaned on one elbow and said, "Well, I'm telling you right now from this bed, you'd better be ready, 'cause on this night you're going to meet Jesus."

"You're a religious nut," said the thief. "I have a notion to shoot you." He barely finished his words when Granny said, "Jesus, sick 'em!"

+ + +

Next day, Granny and Jesus were on the front page of the Hazleton Times, and that evening Granny and Jesus were both on the Tucker Carlson Show. It was such a fascinating story that it was rebroadcast all over the world.

Millions of people heard about Jesus—many for the first time!

Chapter Two

The Motivator

The Shipshewana Bulldogs were known as the graveyard of football coaches. The school consolidated in sixty-five, and for the next ten years produced the longest losing streak in the history of Indiana state football. During that time, they went through seven football coaches compiling a four and seventy-six record. The last time they won—two years ago, the town held a parade and feasted the team with steak and pizza—all the pizza they could eat. Never mind that their opponent, the Connersville Tigers, had their entire offensive team decimated by measles. Rather than cancel the game, Connersville played second stringers.

"Our cheerleaders could beat Shipshewana," they said.

The Shipshewana fire department had other plans. Sensing the opportunity for victory they drenched the field two hours prior to kickoff. It was a virtual mud bowl. No one could stand up. Even the referees were covered with mud from slipping and sliding. Uniforms were indistinguishable and Shipshewana won six to nothing when a Connersville player scooped up a fumble and ran the wrong direction—scoring for Shipshewana! It set off such a celebration that a visitor would've thought Shipshewana had won the state championship.

Afterwards, Connersville filed a protest over field conditions. Shipshewana forfeited the game. The Shipshewana school board, after further investigations, fired the coach who had donated one hundred dollars to the fire department for their assistance. Town folks in an uproar called for the resignation of the school superintendent and vowed to vote out all board members at the next election. Meanwhile, the coaching position was open. No one applied. No coach in his right mind would go to Shipshewana. Football at Shipshewana was doomed. That is, until Dr. Theodore K. Pridgett applied. The script of circumstances that followed could not have been written by even Mel Gibson. Who would've imagined that Dr. Theodore K. Pridgett would change football forever at Shipshewana. Some folks, even to this day, speak of Dr. Theodore K. Pridgett, and the season of seventy-six with reverence. It was their year in history—a season to remember.

July, 1976

The Country-table Coffee Shop was the gathering spot for news and views—mostly gossip. Shipshewana locals gathered there every morning for breakfast. Over the breakfast menu they discussed religion, politics, sex—and, or course, football. The need for a football coach. It was the middle of July and time was running out. Football practice was slated to begin in two weeks—with no coach in sight. The school superintendent announced that a coach had to be hired in one week, or football would be dropped in favor of soccer. The Shipshewana Gazette responded—they ran an editorial denigrating soccer as a sissy sport compared to football. Letters to the editor followed echoing the same sentiments. None, however, offered a solution to finding a coach. It looked like football was doomed in Shipshewana until that morning at the Country-table Coffee Shop.

"Morning Doc, sit down, take a load off. What'd you think about the football program, Doc?" The speaker was Martin Henchen. Henchen ran the Henchen Insurance Agency. He grew up in the area and played football for the old Tomkin Maple leafs, before Tomkin was consolidated into Shipshewana. Henchen, a former lineman, loved sports and never missed a game. It also looked like he never missed a meal and caught a few snacks in between.

"Morning, Doc," said Randy Kaufman before Dr. Pridgett could respond to Henchen's question. Randy operated Kaufman's Hardware and Home Repair Shop. His grandfather started the business, and after his father died, Randy took over. Kaufman's motto: "If we don't have it, we'll get it." His senior year, the first year of the consolidation, Randy Kaufman was quarterback. He still holds the passing record for Shipshewana High. Tall, fast, and smart, he was the ideal quarterback, capable of looking for his receivers over the shorter stocky linemen. His talent was evident even with a losing team. A knee injury, however, in the last game of the season, ruined his chances for a college scholarship.

"Well, what do you think, Doc? We gonna' have a football team, or what?" repeated Martin Henchen.

"I'll tell you what I think, Martin, after I order my breakfast. First things first. You expect me to talk before I get my cholesterol fix."

"I didn't think a Shrink cared about cholesterol. Don't you just sit in your big office and listen to sad stories from disturbed people? said Martin.

CHAPTER TWO

"You forgot, Martin. I was a medical doctor before becoming a Shrink. It's true I listen to a lot of sad stories, from people like Randy here, who keeps reliving his senior year of glory."

"I don't keep reliving my senior year," protested Randy with bacon in his mouth.

"Sure, you do," said Martin. "Doc is right. I've heard you say a dozen times how you came close to beating Connersville, and Richland, and Higby, and if you had it to do over what you'd do to win."

"Well, sure, what's wrong with that?" asked Randy.

"Not a thing, as long as it's kept in proper perspective," said the Doc.

"What's proper perspective?" asked Randy.

"Make an appointment, Randy," said Martin. "The Doc charges for that kind of advice."

"Yeah, well, getting back to the subject," said Randy. "The reason our football team can't win is because our kids are too soft. Those farm boys in Richland County and Connersville just beat the tar out of us. Even little Titusville gives it to our kids."

"Look, Randy, be fair. You only won two games when you were quarterbacking. What right have you to criticize?" said Martin.

"Right—two games! But only six points separated us from winning three others! Of the entire season we were only completely out of two ballgames. With a few breaks, we'd had a winning season—and I remind you it was the first season for Shipshewana. It takes a while for a new school to jell together. Besides, has any team won two games since?"

"No, I grant you that," said Martin. "Fact is, the year after you graduated, Shipshewana started that long losing streak."

"Look here," said Randy handing the Shipshewana Gazette to Martin. "Look at these letters to the editor. They all miss the point."

"What point do they miss?" asked the Doc.

"Just read the letters, Doc. You tell me." Martin pushed the Gazette next to Doc's coffee cup. The Doc began reading aloud.

"The Superintendent has always been opposed to football because he comes from a private school that only played soccer."

"Ouch! Bet that hurt," said Randy. The Doc read some more...

"We want our boys to become men. Football teaches how to compete in life." That statement was signed by a former Marine. All three nodded their heads in agreement even though the Doc never played football.

"If Connersville and Higby, and even little Titusville can have football, and successful football, why can't we?"

"That's a good question, Doc," said Martin…"but keep reading."

"Football teaches discipline. When you get knocked down, you get back up. We need football."

"Sounds like another Marine," said Martin.

"If we don't have football, what will we do on Friday nights—play Monopoly? or Old Maid?" They laughed at that one.

"Not every kid plays football, " said the Doc. "But they should be given the opportunity. Our kids are too soft today and obese. We need to see a Bulldog coming off the field bloodied, but proud that he gave his best."

"I agree with that," said Randy.

"I'm a traveling salesman. If Shipshewana disbands football, I'll not be able to travel to Connersville, Higby, Winston, Titusville, or dreaded Richland. They'll be talking football. What will I be talking about—home economics?" They all laughed.

"Okay, what do these writers to the Gazette miss?" asked the Doc.

"There you go, Doc, don't you shrinks ever do anything but ask questions?"

CHAPTER TWO

"Sometimes we answer questions," responded the Doc. "But it's best if you find your own answer, then you own it. It's yours, not mine. It becomes personal."

"Sure, Doc, sure. I understand," said Randy. "Look, in all these letters to the editor, with maybe one exception, it's the parents who want football—not the kids. Where are the letters from the kids? I tell you they're too lazy and soft today. Shipshewana is a nice neighborhood. Too nice. Our kids don't work for anything like we did. Everything's handed to them: lock, stock, and barrel!"

"Look who's talking—three generations of hardware stores," grinned Martin.

"Hey, I worked hard for my father. As everyone in town knows, Dad was losing the store when he died. Fact is, that's what killed him. I had to borrow money to get it going; put all the inventory on computer, upgraded the stock and remodeled it to keep up with the times. Dad did the best he could, like grandfather before him, but he couldn't keep up in today's world."

"Yeah, I know. Sorry, that was a cheap shot," said Martin. "I apologize. Your father was a good man. He was just competing in a different age."

"You got that. I tried to tell Dad, but he was a hardheaded German, of the old school."

"Getting back to the subject of football," interrupted the Doc. "You're saying our kids are not motivated."

"Correct, Doc. You got it."

"Do you think our kids are softer than Higby kids?" asked Martin. "That's a nice soft plush neighborhood. How come they always have a winning football season?"

"That's a good question, Martin," said Randy. "I'd like to know—how come Higby kids, living in similar economic backgrounds, are more motivated?"

"The answer is obvious," said Dr. Pridgett.

"Obvious? What's so obvious about it?"

"It's as obvious as the nose on your face," said the Doc. "You said it, Randy—it's motivation. Motivation is the key. Higby kids of similar environmental background are better motivated. They are better motivated because they are better coached. The coach makes the difference."

"Am I hearing you right?" said Martin. "Are you saying that of the seven coaches we've had, none of them were worth a grain of salt?"

"No, I'm not saying that at all. For sure, all of those coaches knew the fundamentals of football, but the difference between the Bulldogs and their opponents became obvious by the fourth quarter."

"Oh, now we have another obvious fact," said Randy looking at Martin. "Pray tell, Dr. Theodore K. Pridgett, what is this obvious fact?"

"You go to the games," said the Doc. "You know that we're often leading at halftime. The Bulldogs are always in the game, but in the last quarter they can't reach down, suck it up, and pull it out—and that's the difference in coaching. We've had good coaches, but not motivators. High school kids need to be motivated. Our athletes are as good as theirs, but not motivated. Motivation is the key—the difference. Until Shipshewana hires a motivator, such as me, we will never have a winning football team."

Dr. Pridgett's egotistical suggestion caught Martin and Randy by surprise. They looked at one another, then burst out laughing.

"I know what you're thinking," said the Doc. "You're thinking that the general of the troops has to be an experienced warrior, with a physique like Arnold Swartzenegger. That kind of traditional thinking is dead wrong. Napoleon Bonaparte was not six feet but five feet two inches. Napoleon was a motivator. His troops would follow him to hell and back, if necessary. I'm only five feet eight inches, certainly not your mighty Atlas type, but I'm a motivator. I motivate people every day to turn their lives around, to quit smoking, to quit drinking, to develop self-esteem and confidence. I want people to see that if they can't do it, no one can. The same basic motivational principles apply to football, or any team sport for that matter."

"Are you saying, Dr. Pridgett, what I think you're saying?" Martin's words dripped with sarcasm. "That you, and I emphasize you—that you could motivate this team to be a winner?"

"Is that what you're saying, Doc?" added Randy.

"That is precisely what I am saying," said the Doc.

"Then apply for the coaching job!" Both men said it simultaneously. Both men laughed. Their statement caught the attention of other men at the nearby tables.

"I'm not looking for another job, I'm too busy. Besides, there are motivators out there. Individuals who want to coach football."

"But no one's applying for the job, Doc!" Martin was emphatic and reflected on the desperation of Shipshewana sports fans everywhere.

"Yeah, Doc, where are these motivators?" insisted Randy.

"They're busy making money. Doing other things. Things not so precarious as coaching high school kids to play football. Motivators are no different than anyone else—they want security."

"What do you mean, Doc?" asked Randy.

"You've gone through seven coaches in ten years. That is not security." The Doc had a good point. He drank some coffee and took a bite of his toast.

"They didn't win, Doc!" insisted Martin. "If I don't sell insurance the company fires me."

"Yeah, Doc," said Randy. "The bottom line is winning."

"You're both missing the point. Your company won't fire you Martin because of your attitude. You're motivated. You're a self-starter. As a result of your attitude, your motivation, your persistence, you produce. Your production in sales, like winning—is a consequence, a by-product of your motivation. The bottom line is not winning. Well, it is, but then it isn't. The bottom line is motivation. And proper motivation makes winning a given."

"Doc, let me get this straight," said Martin. "You claim you can take the Bulldogs and make them a winner. You can do it, when seven football coaches, people who live and breathe football, couldn't do it. Am I hearing you correctly, Doc?" His words caused others to stop eating and listen.

"Correct," said the Doc. He ate more toast and took a sip of coffee. "Not only that, with proper motivation, the Bulldogs could win the State championship." Now the whole restaurant was listening and snickering with laughter.

"Come on, Doc, who are you kidding?" said Randy. "For the Bulldogs to win the State, they'd have to have quality players, plus an outstanding coach, and they have neither."

"Plus, a ton of luck," said Martin.

"Wrong," said the Doc. "Luck has nothing to do with anything. I don't believe in luck. We're talking high school here. High school players are still maturing, therefore they're pretty much equal. Sure, some players are better athletes than others, but we're talking about a team concept. In wrestling it's one on one. Basketball even pits five against five, with highly athletic skills. In football, we're talking eleven players on the field at one time. It's a family. They take care of one another. Stronger players with more athleticism, compensate for the weaker ones. It's in the motivation."

"Sounds good, Doc. Theory always sounds good. But the sixty-four-thousand-dollar question is—does it work? "Martin and Randy agreed, and so did everyone else in that restaurant within earshot.

"In the crucible of life experience, my theory works," said the Doctor. "Always has, and always will." He drank his coffee.

"Okay, Doc. You've put your foot in your mouth. Since we have no coach, and in one week, if none shows up—football at Shipshewana is dead. To avoid that, suppose Randy and I put your name up for interim coach, until they can find a good one,"

"Of course, we'll be laughed at, and run out of town," said Randy. The guys on the next table laughed.

"Of course, after all," said the Doc. "What does a bespectacled, one hundred sixty-pound shrink know about a man's game of football?"

"Will you allow us to put your name up?" pressed Martin. "To save football for Shipshewana?" All the guys in the restaurant stopped eating and waited for the Doc's answer. Even the waitress stopped pouring coffee and looked at the Doc.

"No, what did I tell you about security? Full time coaching is bad enough, but interim coaching—there's no security in that."

"Okay, so what do you want, Doc? After all, you don't look like a coach, and we'd have to do a sale job on the school board to hire you." said Randy.

"You're not kidding," chuckled Martin. "It'd be like selling a million-dollar policy!" Everyone laughed.

"I thought the school board was desperate, no coach wanted to come here. Has that changed in the last ten minutes?" asked the Doc.

"No, but you're a psychiatrist. The school board will think we're just stalling to put off soccer," said Martin.

"And you will be," added the Doc. "You don't really think my theories work, do you? None of you do." The Doc looked around at the other customers. No one looked him straight in the eye. They all began eating or sipping coffee. The Doc continued.

"You think I'm just shooting off my mouth. You're hoping to buy time until you can find a real coach." The doctor emphasized the word real, "Am I right?"

"Look, Doc, we like you a lot, but reality is reality. Your theories sound great but I just don't think you're the man for the job. Look at you. Do you look like a coach? What would strapping young high school boys think of you, especially when they find out you never played football? Can't you see that? The traditional concept of a football coach is one who kicks the butt!" Heads nodded as everyone in the coffee shop agreed with Randy.

"I never said I'd be traditional—you're still hung up on traditional concepts. You believe a football coach has to look like Mr. Olympic America."

"No, you wouldn't be traditional!" laughed the men at an adjoining table.

"Well, Gentlemen," said the Doc rising from his seat. "I must get to work. There are people waiting in my office to be motivated—to become winners. And they are paying me big bucks to help them."

"Now wait, Doc. Don't go away mad," said Randy. "I'd like to see your theories put to the test. What kind of security do you want?"

CHAPTER TWO

"I already have security. I'm a doctor, remember? I have patients, and I make big money? Right?" Everyone in the coffee shop agreed about that last point, especially those who had past appointments with the doctor.

"Right, Doc," agreed Martin. "There's no way a school board could offer you the kind of money you're making now. But, Doc, think about this—I think you'd like to see if your theories work?"

"Martin, if you're hoping there is a challenge in that, you're wrong. Dead wrong. I know my theories work. I don't have any doubt about it. The doubt is in your mind, not mine. I know I could guarantee a winner!"

"You could guarantee a winner! Get real, Doc. Guarantee is a mighty big concept. What would be the timetable for this alleged guarantee?" pressed Martin.

"Oh, I'd say the first year, Conference Championship, second year, State Runner-up, and third year—State Champion!" The coffee shop erupted in laughter. The Doc grinned and threw down a dollar bill for tip.

"Are you serious, Doc?" said Randy. "You are serious, aren't you? Doc, either you are plumb crazy, or else the biggest egotist I've ever met."

"To win, one must have an ego," said the Doctor. "Look at Steve Spurrier of the South Carolina Gamecocks."

"Doc, be realistic, no one could take a losing football program like Shipshewana—one that won no games last year, and only four in the last ten years and hope to win the Conference, and the State within three years. It just can't be done," insisted Martin.

"If you say so, Martin. But that's why they're losing. No one expects them to win. And this losing attitude is transported to the boys, so they look for ways to lose."

"You mean they throw the games?" Randy was perplexed.

"Oh no," said the Doc. "They play not to lose, not to win either. Just show up and lose. Because they're supposed to show up and lose."

"Okay, Doc, let's talk turkey." Martin stood up facing the doctor. "What exactly do you want for security? If it's within my power, I'll get it for you. I'll be up front for you—all the way, but you better produce. Are you with me, Randy? And coffee shop people are you with me?"

"Sure, sure, we all are," agreed the people, although somewhat skeptical. Martin said, "Randy, and the rest of us, all want to win. Now if the Doc can produce, I mean right away as he claims, then I say, let's go for it."

"It's agreed, then, Doc. What is it? What will it take?" The entire coffee shop was quiet. No one moved. They wanted to hear the doctor.

"First," said the doctor. "I'm flattered that you asked me. But I cannot allow you to submit my name to the school board. I have hundreds of clients waiting for me. It'd be literally impossible to perform both jobs at the same time. I'd end up in a strait jacket!"

"Doc, we understand your dilemma. We'll ask the school board to be cognizant of that fact and to send a letter to each of your patients, with your permission, as well as to the editorial page of the Shipshewana Gazette explaining that your practice is on a temporary hold for the duration of the football season."

"Just long enough to kill my practice in Shipshewana," added the Doc.

"*Au contraire*," said Randy using his college French. "If you do good—i.e. win, as you say you will, then you'll have people flocking to your office. You'll be turning them away. The entire town will be indebted to you."

CHAPTER TWO

"Remember, I talked about security," said the doctor. "You're thinking of me as an Interim coach—*a temp coach*, If I can put it that way. What kind of security is that?"

"Doc, just tell us what you want?" Everyone in the coffee shop agreed. The situation was desperate. There were no applications and football practice had to start within a week, otherwise the season was lost, along with football forever in Shipshewana. The Doc looked around at everyone. His theories were on the line. Either he had to put up or shut up. It was crazy—he was about to give up a lucrative practice to risk all with a bunch of immature high school boys. What was he thinking—opening his big mouth like that? But he believed in himself. Risk taking is part of life. Besides, his ego was crying out to him. He wanted the adoration—to be known forever as the Vince Lombardi of Shipshewana—a legend.

"Okay, I'll do it," said the Doc. The place erupted in cheers. "But wait a minute, you haven't heard my terms."

"Okay, Doc, what are the terms?" asked Randy.

"I want a one-year contract. I will not take a salary, but the school will pick up all expenses, including lodging for the team at the State finals." That brought laughter!

"Doc," said Randy. "You get the boys to the State finals and the town will book the entire team, and the cheerleaders, in the Ritz." More laughter.

"Plus, all the steak the team can eat," added Martin.

"Secondly," continued the Doc. "I want the town to move old Rodenfelder to the park."

"Rodenfelder, founded Shipshewana," added Randy—"You want to move him?"

"To the park—why, Doc?" Martin and everyone looked puzzled. "No one had ever complained about Rodenfelder before."

"I want him moved to the park. In his absence, I want a bronze life-size statue of me—holding a football. With the inscription: *Coach Dr. Theodore K. Pridgett, Motivator.*

"Wow, don't talk about Steve Spurrier," said a Gamecock fan.

"Doc, I can't guarantee it," said Randy. "The Town Council may have something to say about moving Rodenfelder."

"We're talking about winning the State," said the Doc.

"The State!" Randy was skeptical. "Doc, you win the State, and the Town Fathers will worship the ground you walk on."

"Then Rodenfelder will be moved, right?" asked the Doc.

"Don't worry, Doc. you produce, and Rodenfelder's gone to the park. I'll guarantee it," said Martin.

"Of course, I understand," said the Doc. "We're talking risk here. To motivate, a motivator has to risk all—everything goes on the line, you put the Town on the line; I put my neck on the line. We shall see the results."

"Yep, we sure will, Doc," said Martin. "You'll get your contract, and I look forward to kick off on September 5th with Titusville.

"Yeah, Doc. Don't forget some say Titusville stands for winning titles," added Randy.

"No longer," said the Doc. "From this season on, *Shipshewana is title country—football title country!*"

Boy's Locker Room: Shipshewana high, July 24.

Coach Pridgett looked at his squad and began his talk:

"Men, welcome to the beginning of a championship season. There are 47 of you. Look around, see who is in your family. Some will not be here tomorrow. Some of you will not be here at the end of the season. In future years, because of the tradition that you will build, many more will join you—sixty, eighty, maybe even a hundred will come out for football. This county will become famous for growing football players." He gripped a football. Spun it around and smacked it real hard.

"From this day forward, we are family. And this family is a winner. All for one and one for all. Anyone who even thinks about losing, and expresses that doubt, will be cast out of this family. That person will never play football again at Shipshewana High School. That person will play Monopoly, and Old Maid on Friday nights—not football! you came here as boys you will leave as men." The Doc paced back and forth in front of the boys. Shifting the football from one hand to the other. He gripped the ball and threw it hard across the room straight into a trash can. The ball banged in the can, spun around, and rested on the bottom. The boys were amazed at his accuracy.

"You will know what it means to belong to the family of Bulldogs." said the Doc. "When we go out into the trenches we go out as warriors. We'll be known as the mad Bulldogs of Shipshewana. When you tackle you will swarm like a pack of dogs over its victim. When you grab an opponent, you will hold on—like a bulldog. Teams will learn to fear you. Anyone who catches a pass against you will pay and pay dearly. Quarterbacks will tremble at your barking and feel your bite." The Doc paused.

"Do you sense what I'm saying?"

"Yeah, Coach, we hear you. We're Bulldogs."

"No, you don't yet sense what it means to be Bulldogs, but you will. You will know what it means to be family. Beginning today, all that goes on here—in our family, is private. Secret. No one, not the press, not other students, not your parents, no one will share in these sacred moments of preparation and dedication. Do you understand?"

"Yeah, Coach, what happens in the locker room stays in the locker room."

Doc looked at them. He drank some water from a plastic bottle. Then continued. "Anyone who breaks this trust will be punished before the family and subject to expulsion from the team. Understand!" He waited. You could hear a pin drop. "Now I know what you're thinking. You're thinking what does a little shrimp-shrink know about football? You see, I read the papers too." He walked over to his black doctor's bag. Unzipped it and picked out a scalpel. "Do you see this? It's a scalpel. A scalpel is one of the sharpest instruments in the world. It's used in surgery. Lives depend upon it being sharp. Surgeons do not want a dull instrument."

The doctor walked over to a box and picked up a rabbit by the scuff of its neck. "Do you see this rabbit?" He held up the rabbit. "I'm going to show you how sharp this scalpel is." With one hand he held the rabbit over a pan and sliced the rabbit's throat! The boys groaned, some put their hands over their mouths, others managed nervous laughter. The rabbit kicked, then it was over. The Doc dropped the dead rabbit in the pan and wiped his hands on a towel. The football team, eyes wide open, stared as the Doc continued…

"Do you think this was gross? This was nothing. As a kid I raised rabbits. Rabbits are a dime a dozen. So are football teams. But winning teams—winning teams are rare. My dog killed rabbits. In the past we've been the Shipshewana Rabbits, but no more. The rabbit is dead!"

He reached down into the pan and held up the bloody rabbit! "From now on—we are the Shipshewana Bulldogs, and we kill rabbits!" The team yelled their approval. The Doc startled the kids. He dipped his finger into the bloody pan and tasted the warm blood. "Bulldogs, come, taste the kill. Develop a taste for it. That taste will come—every Friday night!"

September 5th, Shipshewana verse Titusville:

"Men, this is our first game. A lot has been written about this season. A lot has been written about me. Rumors have been flying around apropos my treatment of you. We began with 47 weak players, now we have 37 strong. The weak dropped out. Those who dropped out claimed we used barbaric tactics. They cited the rabbit incident and the blood. They were cowards. It got into the press and put us under a lot of pressure. Some called for my resignation even before the first game! I want you to remember something, we are Bulldogs! Therefore, remember the rabbit. Rabbits are here for the kill, and right now, out there on our field is a field full of rabbits! On our own hunting grounds, we are Bulldogs. What are we?"

"Bulldogs!" they yelled. "Bulldogs!" yelled the Doc. "Bulldogs, let's smash the rumors, and go out there and kill those Titusville Rabbits!"

The team roared from the locker room and ran onto the field. They barked and howled and went through their warmups like a team possessed by demons. They were Bulldogs and the rabbits had come for the kill. Shipshewana people cheered while the opponent's crowd jeered. Someone from the Titusville crowd let a rabbit loose on the field during the Bulldogs warm up. Three Bulldog linemen pounced on the poor creature and broke its neck, then slung it back at the Titusville crowd. Titusville people booed, while the Shipshewana crowd went bonkers. The Bulldogs were mean and hungry. Hungry for the kill!

The Bulldogs kicked off. Titusville fielded the ball on the twenty and a pack of dogs swarmed over the ball carrier for the kill. He never knew what hit him. The ball popped loose into the arms of a burly dog who rambled twenty yards for the touchdown. He spiked the ball and barked like a Bulldog at the stunned Titusville crowd. The Pack, as they called themselves, barked and howled in the end zone. The Titusville ball carrier was carried off the field on a stretcher.

The rest of the evening was a nightmare for the Titusville fans and team. They never got untracked. One after another went down as the Bulldogs ran roughshod over them. The Bulldog's defense was swarming. Titusville never got beyond the forty-yard line. In the second half it was so bad that the Titusville backs dropped to their knees when they saw the Pack coming. Final score—32 to zip.

The Shipshewana people went wild. They'd never seen such spirit, such motivation, such ferocity in their Bulldogs. These Bulldogs were for real. The Messiah had come to town as Dr. Theodore K. Pridgett, and right now, he could walk on water. Randy Kaufman and Martin Henchen couldn't believe their eyes. Surely this was a fluke. "Titusville must be down this year," they thought. The real test would be next week, with the defending Conference Champs—Connersville.

September 12th, Shipshewana at Connersville:

The locker room was quiet. The team had read the papers. All week Connersville had bragged what they were going to do to Shipshewana when they came to town. Editorial after Editorial pointed out that Titusville was down this year, but Connersville was loaded. The Connersville sportswriter had written that the Bulldogs would

CHAPTER TWO

leave town with their tails between their legs—like beaten pups! Coach Pridgett enlarged the article and posted it in the Shipshewana locker room. Now, Coach Pridgett stood before his team, this would be the test. It would not be easy, but nothing worthwhile is easy.

"Men, here we are—Connersville! What we do tonight will determine our future. All week you've read the articles from the Connersville sportswriter. He claims you Bulldogs will get on the bus and leave town like whipped pups! Maybe it's true. Maybe Titusville was down this year. Maybe it was all a fluke!"

"No, Coach, we're for real!"

"Fine," said Coach Pridgett. "Remember, this is a game of execution. If everyone gives 100% in their position, covering their lanes, then we'll win the game. That kind of effort rarely loses. Are you ready, Bulldogs?"

"Yeah, Coach, we're ready!" They yelled in unison.

"Then let's go." They ran out onto the field for warm-ups. The crowd of twelve thousand people roared. About five thousand were from Shipshewana, the rest from Connersville. For the first time, Coach Pridgett was scared, Connersville was big, fast, and mean. Tonight, his theories would be put to the test. He hoped his boys would not be embarrassed. He hoped he'd said the right things and prepared them. The coin toss determined that Shipshewana would receive. Connersville kicked off and raced down the field like a stampede of Buffalo. They hit the Shipshewana ball carrier with such force that the ball popped out—right into the hands of a Connersville player who danced into the end zone. The Connersville people went wild.

It was the beginning of a mistake ridden half for the Bulldogs. By halftime Connersville was up 21 to zip. Shipshewana fans were stunned. Shipshewana looked like the ghost of loser's past! At halftime the Bulldogs locker room was a morgue. Everyone sat silent, licking their wounds. Coach Pridgett stood before his Bulldogs. For Thirty minutes Connersville had put them on a leash and whipped them. Coach Pridgett said nothing—just stared at them for three long minutes. The stillness was broken by a frog that barked his "ribbit" as he hopped from under a bench. Still, no one laughed. It wasn't a laughing matter. They'd choked the first half—or been overwhelmed by a superior team.

Coach threw a towel over the frog and picked it up. "Men, the first half is history. Forget it. We still have an entire second half to play. We can be Bulldogs, or we can be rabbits. He held up the frog. It's entirely up to you. Are you up to it? Can you suck it up? Or will you just croak like this frog?" Then, Coach bit the head off the frog as blood ran down his chin. He threw, no—slammed the headless frog against the locker. "Men don't worry about the score. You come off that field bloodied, and proud, like Bulldogs, and the score will be in your favor! Tackle them so hard they'll think they're decapitated, like this frog." He pointed at the bloody frog on the floor.

"Make them believe! Make them hurt! Act like rabid Bulldogs! Blood dripped from his chin onto his shirt. The team captain jumped to his feet, walked over, picked up the headless frog, and rubbed blood on his lips. He turned and gave a vampirish grin to his teammates. "We're back!" he said. "Kill or be killed!"

Each player duplicated the act. With bloody lips they followed their captain onto the field for the second half. Coach Pridgett knew they were ready.

Shipshewana kicked off to start the second half. They raced down the field like rabid Bulldogs on a mission to bite! Three Bulldogs hit the Connersville ball carrier with such ferocity that it separated him from the ball and nearly decapitated his head. His helmet went flying along with the ball. The ball was scooped up by a Bulldog who rambled into the end zone. The proud Bulldog turned and gave a gosh awful bloody grin to the stunned Connersville crowd. A complete reversal from the beginning of the first half.

Shipshewana kicked off again. The bouncing ball hit a Connersville player trying to get out of the way. The live ball rolled into the end zone and was pounced on by a Bulldog. Touchdown Bulldogs! Connersville never got back into the game. The bus of the Shipshewana players pulled into the parking lot at one o'clock in the morning. To their surprise three thousand fans awaited their arrival! This was the greatest win in the history of Shipshewana sports. Coach Pridgett was king of kings, a miracle worker! He could turn the water into wine, walk on water, and make the weak strong again—and that's what he did for the Bulldogs.

December 7th, State Finals: Hoosier Dome, Indianapolis

The Shipshewana Bulldogs finished with a 10 and 0 season. They'd won the Conference Championship and romped through the sectional and regional meets, holding opponents to ten points or less per game. The Bulldogs averaged 33 points per game over the season. They had been behind only once at half time—the Connersville game. Since that game, and the frog biting, no team had stayed close after the first quarter. Back home, in Shipshewana, Martin Henchen had already contracted to have Rodenfelder moved from the center of town to the park. A cement foundation had been poured in the park and all the town council was waiting on was the State Finals. The entire main street was decorated with Bulldog flags flying from every store. Someone had mysteriously stolen a bronzed Bulldog statue from a company that sold Mack trucks. The bronze Bulldog now stood in front of Rodenfelder in the center of town. Someone draped a sign around Rodenfeldder's neck which read: "*See you next week in the Park.*"

Coach Pridgett and his Bulldogs arrived in Indianapolis for the State Finals. True to his word, Martin Henchen had seen to it that they stayed in the Ritz Hotel. The Shipshewana Bulldogs were facing an upstate team—the Mishawaka Eagles. The Eagles had only lost three games in the last four years. Two of the last four years they'd won the State Finals, a perennial champion with plenty of post-game experience. They were favored to win by every newspaper in the state, except for the Shipshewana Gazette.

The Hoosier Dome, home of the Indianapolis Colts, held upwards to eighty thousand people. For the Friday night game, the Dome would be full. Teams with no post-game experience, and making their first appearance, rarely succeeded. The papers had a field day writing about this temporary coach—a Shrink who'd taken over a losing program to keep football alive in Shipshewana. Now, here they were, facing the toughest team in the state for all the marbles.

Each team was allowed an hour's private practice in the Hoosier Dome to acquaint them with field conditions. Coach Pridgett had his team surround him on the field. "Men, this has been an unbelievable season. No one could've imagined what you accomplished. You've turned football around in Shipshewana and the entire State of Indiana. I'm proud to be your coach. I will be even more proud after you win tonight. We are underdogs. I like being an underdog. No one thought we could beat Connersville, but we did. With the help of a little frog, we won!" The team laughed.

"Now, we face the Mishawaka Eagles. All the sports writers are saying that the Eagles will pluck out the eyes of the Bulldogs. Well, when we get done with the Eagles they will be plucked and cooked tonight!"

"Yeah, Coach!" The team roared their approval. "Years ago, I went out west on a hunting trip. We hunted wolves. You know anything about wolves? They have a strange habit of marking their territory. You know how they mark their territory? By urination. When they want to mark a spot, they urinate on it. Dogs tend to do the same thing. Bulldogs, we're going to mark our territory for the game tonight." The team members chuckled and looked at one another. "So, what are we going to mark, Coach?" And how?" asked the team captain.

"We're going to mark both end zones," said the Doc. "Once we mark them, they belong to us, are you with me?"

"Right Coach, let's do it," they yelled. Coach Pridgett led the team to one end zone. "Okay, men—mark it!"

"How Coach?"

"How? How do you generally relieve yourself? By urination." So, they did, right there, as they gathered in a circle in the end zone and relieved themselves marking the spot. Then Coach took them to the opposite end zone, and they did the same thing. Both end zones were marked by the Bulldogs.

"Men," said Coach Pridgett. "When this game begins, remember both end zones belong to us. The Eagles can have the rest of the field, but the end zones belong to Bulldogs!" The Bulldogs roared their approval and went inside. They were ready. The game was set for kickoff at seven p.m. Kickoff time came and both teams went at it. The game went back and forth. The Mishawaka Eagles rolled up yards but whenever the Eagles reached the twenty-yard line the Bulldogs stiffened and stopped them cold. Twice the Eagles tried field goals. Each time the field goal was blocked. But Shipshewana wasn't much better. Unable to punch it into the end zone, the half-time score was zero to zero.

"Men," Coach Pridgett said, "You have played excellent defense. The Eagles have averaged forty-two points per game. So far, they have zilch! But we must score. We've had lousy field position. We've not gotten beyond our own forty-yard line." Suddenly, the Doc sat down and grabbed his chest. Then he gasped and slumped over. "What's wrong, Coach?" The captain of the team jumped up and ran to him. "Coach, we'll call nine-one-one."

"No—I'll be alright! Just give me a minute. We have a game to play. If you call nine-one-one, it'll delay the game and mess things up for you. You'll lose your edge. You've got to go out and compete and win one for Shipshewana. Remember, we own the end zones."

"Hold on, Coach, we'll win it for you!" The Coach slumped over again. "Coach, you need medical attention!"

"I said, No! Do not call anyone. You guys run out on the field, and I'll ride the golf-cart. Now let's go!" They went out on the field. The coach could barely stand up. Two players held him up as they surrounded him. "Men," he said. "Go out there and win one for this old Shrink!" No trick plays, too late for that. Remember, you own the end zones." He grabbed his chest again. Then slumped down on one knee. "Wet a towel and give it to me," he said. "Men, if I don't last through this game, make it the best darn game you've ever played. Make it one that Shipshewana will talk about for years."

The Bulldogs went out and played their hearts out. Back and forth went the teams until the last four minutes of the fourth quarter. The Bulldogs had reached the thirty-yard line. It was fourth down, they needed seven yards. due to a motion call. The Doc clutched his chest and mumbled to the team, "Go for the field goal. We've got to end this thing now. We can't go into overtime. Bring my kicker here." They brought Billy to the Coach. "Billy, what's the longest kick you've made this season?"

"Thirty-five yards, Coach," said Billy.

"Well, tonight you're going to kick one forty-two or something like that. Now I want you to go out there and smack it right through the center of those up-rights, and once you do that you will be a hero in Shipshewana the rest of your life. No one will ever forget that you smacked that pigskin through the up rights in the State Finals and won the game. Now go do it!"

"Yes, sir, Doc, I'll do it!" And he did just that. They put the ball down on the forty-two-yard line and Billy, said, "Help me Jesus," and kicked it smack through the middle of those up-rights. Shipshewana won the State Championship, just as old Doc. Pridgett shouted, "Thank you Jesus," and slumped over and died.

Billy was indeed a hero, and the town of Shipshewana celebrated for an entire week. While at the same time mourning the loss of the greatest Coach Shipshewana had ever had. A man that they said could walk on water. He had taken a losing team and made State Champions out of them. Signs were placed at both ends of town, right beside the Town Limit sign:

Welcome to Shipshewana,
Home of the Shipshewana Bulldogs,
State Champion of 1976.

And in the center of town, right where old Rodenfelder used to stand, stood a seven-foot bronzed statue of a man holding a football with the following inscription:

Dr. Theodore K. Pridgett, Motivator,
Coach of the Shipshewana Bulldogs,
Indiana High School Champion, 1976.

Chapter Three

The Red-letter Jesus Bible

"A bird in the hand is worth two in the bush; mere dreaming of nice things is foolish; it's chasing the wind."

(Ecclesiastes 6:9; TLB)

Rollie Shaver was eighty, bald, had false teeth, and a wooden leg. He lived with his thirty-two-year-old daughter, Wendy, on twenty-seven acres outside of Beaufort, South Carolina. Wendy's mother had died in childbirth and due to a difficult birth Wendy never had all her marbles, but her daddy loved her and took care of her, and she took care of him. He was a veteran of the Korean War, which was erroneously

CHAPTER THREE

referred to as a Police Action. Yet the Korean War Veteran's Memorial in Washington D.C. listed over 54,000 deaths in that Police Action.

Rollie Shaver was not on the list and the loss of his leg came after the war from a motorcycle accident. He rode an Indian Motorcycle to work each day until the fateful morning he hit a grease spot and skidded across Main Street and under a bus. The bus ran over the cycle and Shaver's leg crushing it so badly it had to be amputated.

It was in 1955 when Shaver got his wooden leg prosthesis, thanks to the Coastal Carolina Bus Company. Their insurance policy paid for it. He had returned to the small farm at Chechessee to be with Windy after the war because he'd trained at nearby Paris Island and fallen in love with the low country. Originally, he was from Frankenmuth, Michigan, but every Marine east of the Mississippi trained at Paris Island. West of the Mississippi they go to Pendleton, California for their training. Rollie Shaver said those were Hollywood marines and weren't as tough. Shaver was better than the Savannah weatherman, and the predictions in Farmer's Almanac. When his missing leg hurt, he said "It's going to rain"—and he always hit it spot on. Before they got an electric drier Wendy would hang the clothes out on a line, and once her daddy's leg started to hurt, he'd say: "Wendy, go gather the clothes up, it's gonna' rain!" He never missed it.

He was not only known as a meteorologist due to the leg, but he was also well known locally as a phrenologist. He knew just about every phrase that had ever been uttered by human lips, and in the course of a conversation he worked them in... *a bird in the hand is worth two in the bush; birds of a feather flock together; the early bird gets the worm; make hay while the sun shines; never look a gift horse in the mouth; out of sigh out of mind, etc.*

Those are just some of the phrases he knew and used. The truth of the matter is Rollie Shaver knew a phrase for each letter of the English alphabet and could usually relate it to low-country common sense for a moral lesson. Another point of fact is most of those phrases, although unknown to Rollie, came from the old King James Version Bible. His favorite phrase, i.e., the one most often used was, *a bird in the hand is worth two in the* bush. Rollie didn't realize that saying came from Ecclesiastes 6:9, or he'd never used it, as he was an agnostic and never understood why God took his wife, and left him Wendy, with an elevator that didn't run all the way to the top.

On this morning, which was like all his other mornings, he was sitting on his front porch in his blue rocking chair and sipping coffee with Wendy. He had a blue rocking chair ever since he'd been at the Cracker Barrel and seen a blue one for sale. He promptly came home, and spray painted his rocking chair with navy blue paint. On overcast days the chair looked black, but on sunny days it was navy blue.

He sipped his coffee and said: "Wendy, it's gonna' rain, my legs acting up."

"Is it gonna' rain, daddy?" she said.

"That's what I said." He shifted his wooden leg just as an old, faded Pontiac pulled into the lane leading back to their house. He watched it and said, "Wendy, a car's coming. Looks like we're gonna' have a stranger."

"Are we gonna' have a stranger, daddy?" repeated Wendy.

"That's what I said," he grunted and leaned over to make sure his shotgun was loaded.

"Are you gonna' shoot him, daddy?" asked Wendy.

"No, not yet—we'll see what he wants."

CHAPTER THREE

The Pontiac stopped and a man stepped out with a baseball cap on his head that read, NRA, and said: "Howdy partner, I'm looking for a Mr. Rollie Shaver, do you know him?"

"And who wants to know?"

"That's my daddy," said Wendy. "Quiet, Wendy," said Rollie as he picked up his shotgun.

"Sir, my name is Emory Morrison, and I'm a Bible salesman."

"A Bible salesman, well, what're you stopping here for?"

Sir, if you're Mr. Rollie Shaver, they told me at the store that you might have some work for me, and the lady there said you needed a Bible."

"Well, they're wrong. I don't have any money to pay for extra help, besides, I thought you said you were selling Bibles. So, what are you—a Bible salesman or a jackleg repairman?"

"Sir, I am indeed, a first-class salesman and a top-flight repairman. If I can't fix it then you don't need it fixed, and I'm selling the latest New King James Version, giant print with red letters for the words of Jesus."

"I don't need any Bibles, and I certainly don't need the words of Jesus, red letters or not. You see Mr. Morrison, I'm what you call an agnostic."

"An agnostic, heavens to Betsy, Mr. Shaver, Providence has led me to the right place."

Wendy looked excited, they hadn't had company for a long time, especially a stranger with a red-letter Bible."

"Daddy, what is a red letter, Bible?" asked Wendy.

"Never mind, Wendy—it's a Bible with the words of Jesus printed in red. And how do you figure, Mr. Morrison, you come in here selling Bibles that I don't need, wanting work that I can't pay you for, and I tell you I'm an agnostic and not interested in your red-letter Jesus, and you're jumping around like a flea on a hot tin roof. Sir, are you deaf and dumb?"

"No, Sir, let me explain. The Bible was written for people like you, an agnostic waiting for more information to come in, like a train pulling into a train station. The Bible I'm selling has that information, and I see you have a gas pump over there for your small tractor or car, while the gutter is falling off your porch roof, and these steps are rotting away waiting for you to fall and break your good leg—I can fix both those things for a few gallons of gas."

Rollie looked at the man. "Look, you come in here with an old beat-up Pontiac and claim you're selling Bibles, and yet have no money. You look like you've been sleeping in those clothes. How do I know whether you might rob me blind? I don't know you from Adam."

"Precisely, and it's a two-way street. How do I know that if I fix your gutter and your steps that you'll give me a few gallons of gas so I can get back to North Carolina. I'm stepping out on the good graces that you're a man of his word?"

"Oh, I'm a man of my word, alright," Rollie Shaver straightened out his wooden leg and stared down at Morrison standing two feet below the porch at the bottom step which was rotten and needing paint. He spoke to him like a judge pronouncing sentence: "You fix those rotten steps, the guttering, all to my satisfaction. Then, once the job is completed, you can have twenty gallons of gas."

"I need to fill up my tank," said Morrison firmly.

"How much does that old Pontiac hold?" asked Rollie.

"Bout thirty gallons," said Morrison. "And I'll start first thing tomorrow morning."

"Tomorrow morning? What's wrong with making hay while the sun is shining?"

CHAPTER THREE

"Sir, as you can see. It's going to be raining shortly and I can't rip off that guttering with the rain pouring down or fix the front porch steps in a downpour. Besides, I need some nourishment first and rest, so I'll have all my energy tomorrow."

"Gosh darn, if you aren't the negotiator," said Rollie. "I'll have Wendy fix you a baloney sandwich but you ain't sleeping in this old house."

"Never meant to," said Morrison. "Baloney is fine. When you're in Rome you do as the Romans do. I'll be fine sleeping in the back seat of the old Pontiac."

+ + +

They went inside and sat around the kitchen table as Wendy fixed baloney sandwiches and poured some lemonade. Morrison noticed she had short shorts on, and strong bronzed pretty legs. "Is that your daughter?" asked Morrison. "Is she married?" He asked and kept looking, without waiting for an answer.

"No, and she's not looking," said Rollie.

"Just asking. You are most fortunate to have her, Mr. Shaver."

"Tell me, again," said Rollie ignoring Morrison's comments about Wendy. "Are you making any money selling Bibles? It's not like you're selling what everyone needs—like pancakes."

"Oh, but Sir, everyone does need a Bible," said Morrison. "It's just the times. Today you can go to an App store on your smart phone and dial up anything you want, even a red-letter Jesus Bible in the latest version."

"Daddy, what is a red-letter Jesus Bible," Wendy asked a second time.

"Never mind," said Rollie. "So, as a Bible salesman you're starving? What did you do before selling Bibles?"

"I sold typewriters," said Morrison.

"Wow, you're running a day late and a dollar short," said Rollie. "What before typewriters? Were you planning a safari for hunting dinosaurs?"

"I sold encyclopedias!" Rollie laughed.

"Man, are you sure you weren't in Saudi Arabia selling snow shovels? What you need is someone to advise you on your next career choice."

"I've had a run of bad luck," agreed Morrison. "But I foresee that things are about to change." He finished his baloney sandwich and drank his lemonade.

+ + +

That very night Mr. Morrison arose like a thief in the night at 3 a.m. Pushed his Pontiac over by the gas pump, and quietly filled the tank to the brim, plus a gallon gas can besides. Then he placed a new King James Version giant red-letter Jesus Bible at the front door with a note, so Mr. Shaver wouldn't miss it: "*What you did for the least of these you did for me.*"

Then he started up the old Pontiac, sped down the dirt lane, turned into the hard surfaced road, and headed north—back to North Carolina. And he was gone!

Chapter Four

Blue Ice Patrol

It was the second week of June, 1973, when Billy, Gregory, and Rodney lay on Paradise Island in the middle of Lake Papakeechie. They lived on Providence Point and had unhooked the flat bottom boat and rowed out to the island. Lying on the ground, shirtless and barefoot, they vowed not to crack a single book the entire summer. They were free. Three whole months of doing nothing but indulging in the sin of idleness. The boys decided right then and there on Paradise Island, to ignore the Presbyterian teaching that *"idle hands are the tools of the devil."* Lying there, looking up into the clear blue Georgia sky they saw two jet streams, heading toward one another. If their destinations continued, they would crisscross directly over the lake. At least, it looked that way from their perspective on the island. The three boys were not prepared for the unprecedented events that followed which would change the entire summer and affect their lives forever.

Chief Papakeechie was from the Siouan speaking Winnebago's who originally inhabited the area. Papakeechie, a thoroughly political creature, immediately saw the wisdom of converting to Presbyterianism; had he not converted nothing would've been named after him. Chief Waccamaw, well known for his integrity and honesty as a neighboring chief, had a larger tribe and covered more territory than Papakeechie, but refused to be converted by the Presbyterians. Chief Waccamaw said the Presbyterians were a bunch of greedy blood sucking land grabbers, using the Great Spirit to justify their thievery of the land. For his refusal to compromise, Chief Waccamaw was ostracized and pronounced a pagan by the Presbyterians, to this day no one knows where his bones lie. Meanwhile, the converted Papakeechie, a known drunk, has a lake named after him.

The name Papakeechie means *Father of waters*, as its water supply came from nearby wetlands and five springs within the lake itself. Papakeechie and his Winnebago's lived off the fecundity of this area which once was teeming with wildlife. It was this same abundance of hunting and fishing that first attracted Presbyterians to the area. However, after a decade or two of exploitation, the early settlers, influenced by Presbyterian theology, recognized the need for stewardship. Once the lake was completed and lots sold all around its ten kilometers, covenant restrictions were passed by what was called the *Papakeechie Homeowners Association*. The Presbyterians wanted a quiet lake, akin to nature, so motors were prohibited, even electric motors. From time to time someone would bring up something to invalidate these restrictions as you can't keep everyone happy all the time. Any effort to change the restrictions required 50% of the homeowners, and the petition would be printed on a ballot and sent to all homeowners. To revoke a restriction required 100% of the homeowners. Rodney's father said that the

Lord would return before these Presbyterians would agree that even a lake existed! It was rumored that "If the angel Gabriel blew his trumpet and asked how many want to go to heaven? He'd never get 100%! "Meanwhile, these restrictions remained, and without motors there'd never be any skiing on Lake Papakeechie. In all this the fish flourished. They grew big and multiplied and loved the quiet unpolluted waters of Lake Papakeechie.

+ + +

The jet stream was quite visible now and penetrated the cloudless blue sky like a giant white marker. As the boys watched the jet airliners crisscrossed, and one of them dropped a blue object. Even from their distance the object looked round, perhaps several feet in diameter. It hurtled toward earth leaving a bluish stream in its trail. Billy yelled, "A meteorite!" But before anyone responded the enormous object hit the lake with a mighty thud, Fifty yards from Paradise Island. At its point of entry, water splashed sixty feet into the air. The boys jumped up, ran to their boat, and rowed to the object, that now bobbed on the surface like a giant blue cork.

"Doesn't look like a meteorite to me," Rodney said. They rowed around it.

"How many meteorites have you seen?" asked Gregory.

"None, but this one's blue and mushy, like ice." Rodney touched it. Poked it with his oar.

"It is ice," said Billy, "And it's melting fast." He reached over and touched it with his hand.

"It's ice, Dummy—blue ice!" Billy repeated.

"Blue ice, what's blue ice?" asked Gregory.

"Who knows," said Rodney. "It must've come from one of those planes, If we don't get it out of the lake it's going to melt."

"Yeah, it's melting fast," said Billy. "Probably melted a lot during the fall."

"Billy, hold the boat steady while we get it on board." Rodney and Gregory jumped into the lake and maneuvered the blue ice next to the boat.

"Okay, Greg, lift and push on three." said Billy. "One, two, three—push!" The ball of ice rolled into the boat.

"Alright!" They high fived and scrambled on board with Rodney. "Head for home, it's melting fast," they yelled. Time was of the essence to save it.

"What are we going to do with it?" asked Gregory.

"Put it in a plastic bag and into the freezer, then we'll figure out what to do with it," suggested Rodney.

"Whose freezer?" Billy asked.

"Dad's" said Rodney. "We've got the space." Rodney's father had an old freezer in the basement for keeping fish.

"Wonder why its' blue?" asked Gregory. It had dark bluish spots and bluish streaks."

"Who knows? Must be special ice served to those in first class," guessed Rodney.

"Taste it, Gregory," urged Billy. Gregory could be tempted to do anything. Gregory rubbed his finger on the ice, scraped off some of the mushy part, and put it to his mouth. His eyes got big as saucers.

"Yikes! This stuff's crap!" He yelled and stuck his head over the side of the boat. Frantically he washed his mouth out with his fingers. Billy and Rodney looked at one another. A fiendish tickle crossed their faces as Gregory gargled with lake water. The boys tried hard to hold their

CHAPTER FOUR

laughter because Gregory had a temper. Billy stopped rowing as both boys shielded their faces with their hands, unable to control it any longer; they burst into laughter which echoed across the quiet waters of Lake Papakeechie. Then came, a riotous, tempestuous belly whopper. The boat rocked with laughter.

"What's so funny?" asked Gregory, as the blue ice trickled down his chin and on his chest.

"You are," they said, pointing to Gregory's chest.

Gregory took one look at the blue streak on his chest and rolled backwards into the lake. Rodney and Billy roared with laughter, but quieted when Gregory popped to the surface and pulled himself back into the boat. They sat there, looking at one another like silent Roman sentinels and stared at the ball of blue ice. Gregory started it first; a painful expression came across his face that soon gave way to hilarity. He couldn't contain himself and absolved the boys from all restraints when he said, "It's salty."

That did it, they lay back in the boat and let her rip. It was a good laugh. A wholehearted belly whopper. It ceased at last, long enough for Billy to attempt to row. Then it broke out again. Billy clung to the oars, laughing and rowing with one hand. Getting nowhere fast. The boat rowed in a circle. Finally, they calmed themselves and Billy wiped his eyes and spoke, "I think I know what this stuff is."

"What?" Greg and Rodney asked simultaneously.

"You hit the nail on the head Greg," said Billy. "You said it was salty and crap. Notice how this ice is blue with dark streaks in it. That blue is the toilet bowl cleanser, Greg. I hate to tell you this, but you just tasted the waste flushed from an airplane toilet!" The expression that filled Gregory's face was the same as when he got an F on a math test. His coloring was like the day his dog Jason got crushed by a cement truck.

He turned and threw up his entire breakfast on the lake—bacon and egg and Apple Raisin Crisp.

Billy rowed again as Gregory lay limp, like a dead man on the edge of the boat, both hands dragging in the water. The boat slowly pulled away from his floating breakfast as fish nibbled the remains.

"Wonder how it got into this frozen ball?" asked Rodney, touching it with his big toe.

"They probably flushed the toilet into a tank or container," said Billy. "It's such a high altitude that it freezes, especially if it's dumped out."

"I didn't think they were allowed to pollute?" said Gregory.

"Maybe it was an accident; the container malfunctioned and dumped it. But who's to know? It melts on the way down, only this one didn't melt.":

"Yeah, and if we hadn't been on the island it would've fallen into the lake and melted, and no one would've known." The boys docked at the pier and put the blue ice in a Hefty trash bag, then carried it to the basement There they stashed it in the fishing freezer. "We've got to figure out what to do with it," said Rodney. "I don't want my mom to find it. Let's go down to the store and get a drink and think."

"I've got to brush my teeth," said Gregory as he jumped on his bike. "See you at the store." Greg's teeth looked bluish. The boys laughed and rode to Martin's Quick Shop.

+ + +

Eden Park Mall was a favorite hangout during the summer months. Behind Martin's was an acre of shady trees and a picnic area with a pavilion. Eden Park with its picnic pavilion was a popular place for family reunions and garage or bake sales. Beyond the park was the earthen dam

CHAPTER FOUR

that held back the waters of Lake Papakeechie. Martins also had a Bait & Tackle shop next to the store, and of course, Bob's Clip Shop with the old wooden Chief Papakeechie standing in front of the small shopping center. The Mall was a communications center for the lake with a bulletin board for announcements that ranged from help wanted to sale items for special events—like the Papakeechie Homeowners Association.

The boys walked over to the wooden Indian, rubbed his nose and waved to Mr. Bob inside. Then they went into Martin's and bought candy and drinks. While waiting for Gregory to arrive, they read the bulletin board. "Look at this," Rodney said, "They need ice, and we have ice—blue ice. This plays into our hands. Our blue ice is manna from heaven sent by God!"

"Or the devil," Billy added. They stared at the announcement for the annual Lawn Party and Craft Sale sponsored by the Papakeechie Homeowners Association. Proceeds would be for tree planting in Eden Park, chemical weed treatment of the lake, fish stocking and road restoration around the lake. And at the end it stated that they needed ICE.

"Mr. Martin," Billy said. "I see you're having a lawn party and craft sale on June 14th."

Mr. Martin was a big man. A Viet Nam war hero. He'd lost one leg by stepping on a land mine. He'd spent months in a VA Hospital in Arizona. Then was transferred to the Methodist Hospital in Indianapolis for a prosthesis and rehab. Like most vets he never talked about Nam, but on rare occasions would be willing to show us his artificial leg. Rodney had seen it twice and had started to touch it, but Mr. Martin wouldn't allow touching. The boys were fascinated by that artificial leg and spent hours talking about it, that he could feel the missing leg and say, "My legs acting up, it's going to rain!" They couldn't figure out how he could feel anything in a missing leg—but he did! And his predictions were always right on!

"That's right, Billy," said Mr. Martin responding to Billy's question about the Lawn Party and the need for ice. He limped around the counter toward the boys. He walked great with the leg but still there was an obvious limp, or some kind of funny artificial knee jerk type of movement. "You boys want to help?"

"If we could," said Billy.

"Well, that's great boys. I'm mighty proud to hear you volunteer. I have people telling me that our young people are going to the dogs. Wait 'till I tell them this."

"Why do you need ice, Mr. Martin, since you sell bags of ice out front?"

"Ice? Well boys, they need a lot more ice this year because this is the 50th Anniversary of the Lake, and we'll have bigger crowds than in the past, and the homeowners will need more than a couple bags like I've donated in the past. Besides, this year they're serving a special punch. Fact is, I'm going to tell you boys a secret, and it'll knock your socks off—it's a blueberry punch!"

"Blueberry punch," Billy and Rodney responded together like the audience in the Presbyterian Church with a cacophony of sound to Dr. Brown's sermons. Rodney's eyes got big as saucers as he looked at Billy. They both had the same thought; blueberry punch was perfect for the blue ice. It was if the devil himself had walked over and whispered, "Boys, I have a great idea for your blue ice."

"Believe me boys," said Mr. Martin. "I've tasted it, and it's great! You won't be able to get enough of it. They're making it special for the celebration. "

CHAPTER FOUR

"Mr. Martin, Rodney and I, and Gregory too, would like to provide the ice for the punch. We'd make sure the ice is here on time, and in the punch bowl That would save the women from having to worry about it."

"Boys that would be just great—wonderful. I'll tell my wife that you boys will get the ice. Now you won't forget, and you'll get the ice here on time. Don't want any screwups!"

"No Sir, Mr. Martin, no screw-ups. We'll make sure that the ice is right here, and ready for the punch."

"By golly, that's great," said Mr. Martin. "I'm going to tell everyone what fine boys you are. I can't get over that you're volunteering like that. I'll tell you what I'm going to do. The rest of the summer whenever you boys get hot and need a soda, come see me, but don't tell the other kids. You hear?"

"We won't Mr. Martin. Does that include Gregory too? He's helping us with the ice."

"That includes the three of you for taking care of the ice problem. "

The boys left the store elated. It was too good to be true. The blue ice was destined for the 50th Anniversary of the founding of Lake Papakeechie. This gift had just dropped out of heaven, like manna, into their grimy idle hands, almost as if Providence had ordered it. Or was it the devil himself? Time would tell. Regardless, the boys were on a roll, an ordered roll with destiny.

+ + +

It seemed like June 14th would never come. Three times a day the boys went to the fishing freezer, opened the plastic bag, and religiously turned the frozen ball checking to see that all was well. One afternoon, a storm came up, knocking out the electricity for an hour. It threw them into a tizzy thinking the blue ice might melt. it didn't.

Thanks to Mr. Martin the boy's reputation grew. Like an evangelist he enthusiastically spread the word of their volunteering. Mr. Martin, like other fishermen around the lake was prone to exaggeration. Overnight, the three boys became celebrities; parents held them as role models. Whenever a child around the lake got into trouble, the parent would say, "Why can't you be like Rodney, Gregory, or Billy?" It became so bad that kids hated their names. No one could live up to such reputations. Despite these platitudes, not once did these three boys flinch from discarding their infamous plan. The blue ice would be used. The closer the 14th came, the more determined and excited they became. It was like being driven or possessed to carry out their fiendish plot. On top of this, each of those boys had the blasphemous audacity to kneel by their bedsides at night and give thanks to God for the blue ice—as if Providence had ordained this impending atrocity.

+ + +

Finally, the day arrived. Banners were unfurled around the lake. Eden Park buzzed with excitement and flags marked the lakes 50th Anniversary. Tents were set up and tables laden with crafts, baked goods, and yes, even history. A special tent was designated as the historical center. It had scrapbooks filled with pictures and the original charter of Lake Papakeechie. Also on exhibit was the original Papakeechie seal of Judge Josiah Cunningham, a staunch Presbyterian and charter member.

Judge Cunningham, known as the hanging judge, was retired, but still active and had all his marbles at ninety-one. Well, maybe most of them. He arrived promptly at seven a.m. and sat in the historical tent to

CHAPTER FOUR

await the festivities. He looked as old as Methuselah. In the center of this tent was the punch bowl and a cake that marked the 50th Anniversary of Lake Papakeechie. All visitors would come in, browse around, meet the judge, have a piece of cake, and indulge in the Papakeechie ladies' special blueberry punch. This special event of cutting the cake and serving the punch would take place precisely at ten o'clock. It would be introduced by the President of the Homeowners Association.

The night prior to the Anniversary the boys slept together at Rodney's house—close to the ice. They were so excited they couldn't sleep. Who could sleep at such a time? They arose at six a.m. and by seven had packed the blue ice into an ice chest, surrounding it with dry ice. The next two hours seemed like eternity. The three of them sat yoga style, watching the chest and the clock. Billy, always thinking, called it "Joshua time," as it appeared that the sun stood still. Finally, the time arrived. At nine o'clock they rose up like pallbearers and marched to Eden Park bearing their prize. They marched through the crowd to whispers of praise and admiration—straight to the historical tent. They were on an evangelistic mission with the blue ice. Once they saw the punch bowl, they knew they had a problem. It was too small for the chunks of blue ice.

Undaunted, Billy said, "Greg, go borrow a hammer from Mr. Martin." In no time flat, Gregory secured the hammer and they split the ice into four chunks—four ugly chunks.

"Yuck, what's that?" Gregory pointed at the bluish-brown streaks embedded in the chunks.

"Looks like some kid had diarrhea," said Billy. "We'll use this chunk first, put it in the punch bowl upside down, with the pretty blue on top!"

The ladies poured the punch into the bowl and were ready for the ice. "Okay, boys, do your thing and put in the ice. We want the punch bowl to be good and cold. People will be coming for our special blueberry punch at ten o'clock."

"We're ready, Mrs. Martin," Rodney said. "We have what we call blue ice from heaven. "

"Well, my word, ladies—look at this. I never saw blue ice before. Don 't suppose that will affect our blueberry flavoring?" Mrs. Martin looked skeptical.

"No ma'am," Rodney assured her. "It's just food coloring. We checked with our moms. That's why this is so special. We call it blue ice from heaven."

"My sake, you boys are something special. Food coloring—how ingenuous. She echoed our lie and all the ladies smiled and wanted to touch us as if petting a puppy for good behavior.

"Yes, ma'am," Rodney repeated. Billy and Gregory put the chunk of blue ice in the punch bowl using clear latex gloves to impress the ladies. They put the remaining ice in the huge vat with the rest of the punch which contaminated the entire batch. Satisfied the deed was done, no turning back, they waited. The waiting was killing. When you're about to pull off the most mischievous deed in the history of the lake, the waiting is killing.

"Joshua time," Billy repeated.

At precisely ten o'clock, the President of the Homeowner's Association gave a boring ten-minute speech. It seemed like an hour. "More Joshua time," said Billy. Then the old Judge stood up and reminisced for another ten minutes, interspersed with his hacking and coughing.

"The blue ice will kill him," whispered Billy.

"It nearly killed me," said Gregory.

Finally, the speeches over, the President invited everyone in the tent for punch and cake. Then the devil took over. He grabbed the boy's plan

CHAPTER FOUR

and ran with it. They could not have planned it any better. This great historical moment in the history of the lake; a moment which would render these boys famous for life, and make them, forever the envy of their peers…

"Ladies and Gentlemen, boys and girls, before we go any further, the ladies of Papakeechie have prepared a special punch for our celebration. We presently have ten members on our Homeowners Board of Directors, plus me the president, and Judge Cunningham. We twelve will drink a toast to Lake Papakeechie and her future. Then, we invite each of you to indulge with punch and cake."

"Wow, this is too good to be true," said Gregory.

"Yeah, history in the making," said Billy.

The ladies of Papakeechie with proper decorum served up the punch to the Board of Directors, all ten of them, along with the President and old Judge Cunningham. They stood holding the cups of punch.

"To Papakeechie," said the President.

"To Papakeechie," said the Board of Directors and the Judge. Down the hatch went the punch! The boys silently watched, like the devil at the crucifixion.

+ + +

Those Board members stood there, silent for a fleeting second or two, with the most painful expressions. Color drained from their faces and all twelve Board members exhibited enlarged moon pie eyes, raised eyebrows and human geysers about to blow. It was in that split second of time that Billy cracked, "the blue ice is working."

The Judge went first. He spewed blueberry punch ten feet into the crowd with his false teeth flying. The President of the board went next, spitting and hacking; then a trail of the blue ice ran down his chin and a gob of dark stuff hung from his mouth. These shocking expressions went right down the line, like dominoes through the entire Board of Directors. One after another, or simultaneously, they spit, coughed, and spewed forth vituperations that no good Presbyterian should know.

The old Judge fell on the ground and rubbed his gums with his fingers in a futile attempt to erase the gosh-awful taste from his mouth. The President made a mad dash for the earthen dam and jumped straight into the lake in a wild attempt to clean his mouth of the abomination. The proper ladies on the Board hiked their skirts and rubbed furiously at their mouths, turning in circles, and damning the culprits responsible. The male board members stomped, coughed, and yelled like savages and behaved like the non-elect. The ladies who served the punch fainted, one after another like dominoes falling. It was a scene like never before or since—Judge wallowing on the ground, President in the lake, board members wailing like banshee spirits, and more cursing than when the devil was kicked out of heaven. It was a day to be remembered and the boys took in every glorious moment with such riotous hilarity that it was obvious to all that they were guilty as sin.

Ironically, in those few fleeting seconds of raw confusion, adults who formerly looked upon the boys as heroes now saw them as villains, while the young people exalted them as legend. The men in the crowd grabbed and held them, eager to strangle their skinny necks. "Rip off their pants and beat the tar out of them!" Yelled an anonymous voice from the crowd. This was seconded many times over and the boys got a good shaking when the Judge came to his senses and spring to his feet, coughing all the time. He retrieved his teeth and acting as Judge and Jury tried the three boys on the spot.

CHAPTER FOUR

"What the Sam-hill did you boys put in that punch?" he yelled. A patch of dark stuff hung from his mouth.

"Blue ice, Sir," Rodney said, unable to contain himself. A man began shaking him.

"What in God's name is blue ice?" said the Judge. "And where did you find it"

"It came from heaven, Sir," said Rodney, losing it again and more shaking followed.

"Heaven my eye, that stuff came straight from hell and you boys have the devil in you!" The Judge trembled and was on the verge of another collapse. He wiped his mouth. His teeth were clacking. "This gosh darn blue stuff is straight out of hell," he repeated.

"No, Sir, it came from the sky," said Billy. "An airplane dumped it out. It's toilet bowl waste, Sir!" All three boys burst out laughing again and got another terrific shaking for it.

"Toilet bowl waste," said one of the proper ladies on the Board of Directors. "May God help us!" She fainted. Another female member of the board, suspected of her bulimia, vomited without any self-inducement.

The old Judge bent over in pain and blew his teeth out again. His teeth were stained with blue streaks. The Judge rose up, shook, and muttered indistinguishable words while slimy feces and mucus dripped from his chin.

"My God, boys, you've killed the Judge!" yelled a bystander. This was an obvious lie as the Judge was still standing; shaken but standing!

Seeing the Judge like that caused the boys to lose it again. They couldn't help it. The blue ice had smitten the Judge with temporary insanity. Every kid in Eden Park started laughing, and Rodney, Gregory, and Billy became gods to them. Two, four, seven kids, got a whipping right there on the spot for laughing. It was too late; however, the damage was done, every kid wanted to be like those three boys. The parents were furious, and it looked bad for the boys safety until the Judge came to his senses once more.

"You guys will pay for this. You owe every person around this lake an apology for your devilment. What grade are you boys in?"

"Seventh grade, your Honor," said Billy.

"Seventh grade, I can't believe this. People, our kids are going to the dogs, and this is a prime example. Where are your parents?"

"They're working, your Honor," said Rodney. Billy's mother had come, proud that they had volunteered to help, but now, with this turn of events, she slipped to the back of the angry crowd and disappeared. Lest we judge her harshly for cowardice, just think, would you have claimed these boys?

Someone retrieved the teeth for old Judge Cunningham. "Boys," the Judge said, his blue teeth clacking. He pointed his shaky finger at all three boys—a finger still dripping with bluish slime. "You boys will travel to every house around this lake during the next two weeks and apologize for this devilment! Not only that, but you will also serve ten community hours for every board member victimized by your ungodly blue ice. And that includes the President over there in the lake, and me, a total of one hundred twenty community hours! Each recipient of your devilment will determine their own ten hours of service for you, and the service will be rendered to their satisfaction. As far as I am concerned, you boys are on probation the rest of the summer, and the slightest hint of any altercation, any complaint, and you boys will be turned over to the County Youth Services Commission."

"Hear, hear," said the crowd with approval.

"Throw it to them, Judge. These delinquents have got to learn we don't cut any slack!"

CHAPTER FOUR

"Not only that," continued the Judge. He was fit to be tied and, on a roll now. "You boys will henceforth be designated as the Blue Ice Patrol. This will not be a designation of honor but of shame. Shame on you for serving up that gosh-awful stuff and ruining our celebration. Your names will live on in infamy as the boys who ruined the 50th Anniversary of our splendid lake. Now I know that time has a way of healing things and erasing memories, therefore, to ensure that your devilment is never forgotten, your names will be placed in the Board of Director's minutes. The three of you will forever be known as members of the infamous Blue Ice Patrol."

"Hear, hear," echoed the crowd.

"So be it, way to go, Judge!"

They released those boys and the crowd parted as they walked through their midst like Israelites fleeing the Egyptians at the Red Sea crossing. They moved cautiously, in the presence of clenched fists and bitter shouts. "The Blue Ice Patrol, the Blue Ice Patrol. You boys are members of the dang Blue Ice Patrol!"

And so it was, just as the old Judge had said it would be. Rodney, Gregory, and Billy became known as the Blue Ice Patrol. To adults they were the epitome of bad boys, destined for prison. Overnight, the former looks of admiration had turned to glaring bitterness. As of June 14th, the cookies and milk had dried up. But to their surprise, the young people, all around the lake and surrounding area looked upon those three boys as gods. And before the summer was over, their peers held them in such high esteem, like Jesus, they could even walk on water. It was a summer never forgotten by the Blue Ice Patrol. It was a summer that revealed to those boys that one foolish decision might easily brand you for life.

Chapter Five

Out of Egypt

Rufus Ray Roberts had been brow beaten for forty tiring nagging years when he decided to do something that no protestant would ever consider doing—he went to a priest. Rufus was tough. It would never be said of him that he gave up easily. He was a survivor of the old school. He did not believe in divorce. He took Jesus at his word, "Whoever divorces his wife for any reason other than sexual immorality causes her to commit adultery and whoever marries that woman (the one divorced for any reason) commits adultery." Those red-letter words of Jesus burned on his brain. He could not divorce his wife for any reason other than sexual immorality. And he knew his wife would never cheat on him. And he'd never cheat on his wife, but she would, and had, beaten him to death with her nagging. There's more than one way to kill a man. After forty years a steady rainfall will wear away even a rock,

CHAPTER FIVE

and Rufus was a rock who'd withstood a steady downpour of forty long endearing years. Now, enough was enough,

The solution was inevitable—go to a priest and hope for a truce, at least a progressive denuclearization of the fiery weapons of nagging. Rufus could not take his case to his own pastor for one simple reason—she played the pipe organ and no pastor in his right mind is going to upset a pipe organ player, since they're as rare as dinosaurs. Ridgeland was not Jurassic Park where organ players could be hatched from DNA. If the priest did not have a Dr. Phil plan, then Rufus might have to bite the bullet and kill his wife. That was the last alternative since such action would throw him into direct conflict with more red-letter Jesus words like "You have heard it said, thou shalt not murder, but I say whoever is angry with his brother without a cause is in danger of the judgment."

Rufus was fearful of jail. Few people get by with murder. He knew that if he went that far he'd better buy stock in Preparation H. With a possibility of a lifetime of incarceration, he'd need it. Rufus also knew such action would put him afloat on the River Styx to Hell. But what was his alternative, he was already living in Hell! So, on this day, Monday, he'd make his move and visit the priest.

"Where are you going, Rufus?" asked his wife, Maggie. Her name was Marjorie, but everyone called her Maggie. Rufus quietly called her Naggy! Or Magpie! But not to her face, never to her face.

"I'm going out," replied Rufus. He wasn't about to explain to her or disclose to her what was on his mind. It had been on his mind for the last ten years., like a worm devouring his thoughts, like a parasite sucking all the liquid fluid from his brain, like an orange with the juice sucked out.

"Out?" Maggie repeated. "While you're out bring me back some of those newly advertised Nacho Fries from Taco Bell." She flung words at him like a dart as he went out the door. "And mow the lawn when you get back, the neighbors will think we're white trash!"

"Nacho fries—she's big as a drum now, what does she want with nacho fries?" For the last twenty years she'd been expanding, like a never-ending building program—like a cathedral that took a hundred years to build. Twenty years ago, they'd gone to Spain and visited the Cathedral Santiago de Compostela, where allegedly St. James was buried. It had taken over a hundred years to build that Cathedral. The Cathedral of Maggie had taken the last twenty years, and it still wasn't complete. Now Rufus was telling himself "I'm not staying around for the dedication of the building."

Taco Bell was four blocks beyond the Church of St. Francis, so Rufus decided to stop at the church first, to take care of his serious business. He could buy the Nacho fries later and hope that Naggy, or Magpie, or whatever he wanted to call her would have a heart attack devouring those fries. The thought occurred to him to kill her off innocently with artery clogging foods—except it might take too long. He remembered seeing on TV something about "My 600-pound wife."

He walked into the sanctuary. Before him he saw the blessed Jesus on the cross and felt guilty for even being there. Then he remembered her words, "Bring me some Nacho fries!" His bitterness overtook him even in the presence of the blessed Jesus on the cross. It was on his mind and the devil was whispering into his good ear—"kill her, kill the bitch!" He felt like Cain thinking of killing his brother, Able. "Sin is crouching at your door and you need to master it."

He went into the confessional booth and waited. The door had a bell on it that alerted the priest who would come shortly. He sat there, in the confessional booth—in God's waiting room; waiting on the Lord to speak to him though the priest. He thought of Moses and the burning bush. Moses didn't go out that morning hoping to find the Lord. He was looking for his sheep, but instead found the Lord and a pack of trouble. Rufus was looking, in God's waiting room with his shoes on, and then he heard the words.

"What can I do for you, my son?"

"I need help," said Rufus. He got right to the point. No sense wasting the lord's time or the priest. "If I don't get help, I'm thinking about killing my wife."

"Oh, no, my son, you don't want to do that. That is the sixth commandment—thou shalt not kill."

"I know that, Father. I'm aware of that, but my wife has been killing me by nagging the last forty years, and I can't take it any longer."

"Patience my good man. Blessed is the man who perseveres under trial…"

"Father, do you know what it's like to be nagged day and night; no, I'm sorry, I guess you don't know, as you aren't married?"

"My son, you forget we have a school here with twenty nuns—all under my care. In contrast, you only have one to whom you must answer,"

"Father, I am sorry, Sir. But in your situation, you could transfer the bitching ones out to another diocese whereas I can't possibly transfer out my wife."

"That is true, my son. But remember God gave Eve to Adam to test him."

"True," said Rufus. "And Adam failed the test; they were driven out of paradise."

"But as far as we know," suggested the priest, "God was with them even outside of Paradise, and they had many children, do you have children, my son?"

"Yes," said Rufus, "but they are grown, and I'm left to live in the Valley of Gehenna with the daughter of Satan."

"You are not living with the daughter of Satan," said the Father. "You are blessed and don't know it, count your blessings, name them one by one."

"Father, being positive does not work. I have tried to be positive for the last forty years."

"Have you prayed, my son?"

"Prayed? I have cried out like an atheist in a foxhole; no, like a patient in a dentist chair waiting for a root canal."

"And God has heard your prayers and here you are."

"Okay, where is my burning bush; what is God's answer, Father?"

God's answer is plain, my son—go back to Egypt!"

"Go back to Egypt! Father, I've already been enslaved in Egypt the past forty years. Like the children of Israel, I need deliverance—that's why I've come to you."

"Our time is up, my son. Now go back to Egypt."

"Father, you're not listening to me. If I go back, I am seriously thinking of killing her."

"My son, I know you've come to me in confidence, but under the circumstances it is my moral duty to report you to the authorities."

"What? After I've poured my heart out to you? What would you report? After forty years of a quiet marriage, Rufus Ray Roberts is talking about killing his wife. Meanwhile, he has no record, no felonies, nothing, no spouse abuse, no crime has been committed, he hasn't even received a speeding ticket and you want to waltz into a police station and hatch up some God forsaken unbelievable story. Who would believe you?"

"It appears to be my moral duty, as much as reporting child abuse to the authorities."

CHAPTER FIVE

"Oh, child abuse is bad, and you priest know a lot about that! But killing my wife would be good. Eliminating evil from the world."

"My son, you need therapy."

"No, what I need is a plan; that's what I need, a sure-fire plan."

"You know, if your wife comes up missing, the first thing they look at is the spouse."

"Exactly," said Rufus. "That's why I need a plan." He walked out of the confessional booth, waved goodbye to the priest, and strolled out of the church. The moment he waved goodbye to the priest the devil took over his mind—it was like Cain and his brother Abel, "Come on Abel, let's go for a walk! Let's go to the Club for a drink." It was later that Cain killed Abel with a club.

Rufus picked up the Nacho fries and thought to himself, "Nothing will persuade me otherwise. I just need the perfect alibi. He drove home with the Nacho fries." As he walked into the house she yelled: "Well 'bout time, Lord has mercy. Where'd you go, China?"

+ + +

Maggie was looking at a paint chart while awaiting Rufus to return. She thought, "I think a light cream will be nice for the living room, it'll go with the furniture. Hope Rufus returns soon."

The phone rang. "Hello, this is Maggie. Oh, hi Sally, I'm sitting here waiting for Rufus to return, looking at paint charts. I want him to paint a room. It just takes so much nagging to get him to do anything. He is the world's worst procrastinator! And the older he gets the harder it is to get him to do anything. He just doesn't seem to have any energy these days. Oh, yeah, I thought about talking to the pastor about him, but you know, Rufus is chairperson of the trustee Board, and he does so much stuff for the church, but I can't get him to do anything. for me. I'm really thinking about going to a Catholic priest. Why not? It'd be like getting a different or second opinion from someone who doesn't know him. Oh yes, I'm serious. In fact, it's been so bad lately that I'm seriously gonna' stop at that St. Francis Catholic Church. Oh, got to go—here comes Rufus. Bye."

+ + +

The next day, Maggie stopped at the Church of St. Francis. She walked into the sanctuary and saw Jesus on the cross and felt guilty that she and Rufus had been having so many harsh words. She saw the confessional booth and entered; the bell rang for the priest. She waited.

"So, this is what the confessional booth looks like. Feels like I'm in God's waiting room. I wonder if we must wait in heaven. "Take a number and wait," she thought. "Everywhere—take a number and wait." She heard the door open on the other side as the priest entered. She spoke.

"Father, I have a problem."

"What it is my sister?"

My husband is the world's biggest procrastinator, and I don't know how to get him to do anything without nagging, nagging, and nagging him."

"You're killing him with nagging."

"Just about, Father, but he's killing me by ignoring me and putting me off."

"Do you have children at home?"

"No, Father, they have grown up and left the nest, and we sit looking at one another. And sometimes he is so stubborn that you'd think I married Satan Incarnate."

CHAPTER FIVE

"Believe me, Sister, you did not marry Satan incarnate."

"Has he been faithful to you?" the priest asked.

"Always, Father, and he was a good father when the children were growing up. But now he has no energy and puts things off, and I have to nag him to do anything, like washing the car or mowing the lawn."

"Have you been faithful to him?"

"Always, Father, but it's made me so nervous that I eat too much."

"You need to count your blessings and name them one by one."

Father, that's good positive advice but that doesn't seem to work now, it's like we're living as slaves in Egypt."

"Have you prayed about these problems?"

"Prayed? Father, I have cried out like the woman before the unjust judge, like a patient about to have a root canal!"

"Where have I heard that before?" said the priest.

What do you mean, Father?"

"Never mind, I'm thinking," said the priest.

Father, I came expecting an answer like Moses from a burning bush. What can I do, Father?"

"What did God tell Moses at the burning bush?" asked the priest.

"He sent Moses back to Egypt," said Maggie.

"Okay, go and do likewise—go home and be delivered. God will provide a way just like he did with the Israelites in Egypt. Therefore, go back to Egypt."

So, Maggie went back to Egypt and wondered how things could be reconciled with Rufus. How she could get him to paint the room without nagging. She didn't enjoy nagging, no woman does, fact is, it gave her a headache and caused her to eat more. She only knew one woman who enjoyed nagging, and that would be Martha down the street. Martha never stopped nagging. Martha was the quintessential nagger.

Martha had related in their monthly coffee meeting that it's a wife's duty to nag from sunup to sundown, otherwise, the husband becomes an unresponsive nincompoop. Well, that was Martha's strategy, not Maggie's.

+ + +

Maggie met Rufus in the living room. "Come with me," she said, and they moved to the dining table where she sat down to eat her Nocho fries. "Sit down," she said to Rufus, and he obeyed and sat down. "I've been thinking about painting the living room—a cream color. I'd like you to paint it." Rufus grunted. Maggie couldn't tell whether it was an approval grunt or a disapproval grunt. After all these years she should be able to tell. "But painting the room is not what I wanted to talk about." she said. "I've been reading the Bible…"

"You've been reading the Bible," said Rufus looking surprised.

"Yes," said Maggie. "And you know what I've found?" She didn't wait for Rufus to speak…"I've found that Moses was looking for sheep, and instead found God, and God spoke to him through a burning bush. Now, isn't that something?"

"That is something, however," Rufus said, "After all these years in the church you should've already known that."

"I probably did know it, but I forgot it. The point, that I'm trying to make is this—Moses left Egypt and for forty years was living in the desert with this woman that he married. Forty years of relative peace and quiet— then God interrupts his peace and quiet, speaks to him and says, Moses, I want you to go back to Egypt and deliver my people. Rufus, what do you think of that?"

"Well, I think it's wonderful, Moses obeyed God and went back and delivered them. We saw that portrayed in the "Ten Commandments with Charlton Heston."

CHAPTER FIVE

"The significant thing, Rufus is this—the number forty. Moses was forty years in the desert; he had peace and quiet, we've been married forty years, but peace and quiet, maybe not so much."

"I think you're right," said Rufus as he got up to leave.

"Wait," Maggie continued. "I recently went to the St. Francis Catholic Church; do you know why?"

"You went to the St. Francis Catholic church?" Rufus was shocked.

"Yes, and do you know why?"

"No, but I suppose you're gonna' tell me."

"I sure am, I sat in that confessional booth waiting on that priest, like waiting for God to show, and while waiting, this burning bush thing came to me."

Rufus didn't dare tell her that he too, had gone to St. Francis, and he also had waited in that confessional booth."

"Rufus, God spoke to me…no, I did not see a literal burning bush, but I did experience one, and I spoke to the Father. He's a nice man, and I did confess my sins."

"You confessed your sins? Rufus was scared, and afraid, that the priest may have put two and two together.

"And you know what, Rufus? —i don't want any more of these Nocho fries. I've been eating and ballooning up because I'm nervous and unhappy, and well, a bitch!"

Rufus was shocked, I mean really shocked. She called herself a bitch.

"Rufus, there's something we need to do."

"What is that, Maggie?" He was afraid to ask.

"Like the Israelites of old, we need to get out of Egypt. See the world. Forget the paint job; we can do that later. We're getting older, let's enjoy one another and see what God has done. And let's read the Bible together. Do you think we can do that, Rufus?"

"Well, yes—I have to admit I'm shocked. But it's a good shock. I mean, it seems like you really did see a burning bush." Now Rufus felt guilty, and ashamed….

+ + +

"Maggie, I'm ashamed, and also have something to say. I went to St. Francis before you did, and I spoke to the same Father. He said we should count our blessings. I did not see a burning bush, but I did experience the fact that we're in Egypt waiting to be delivered, just like the Israelites under Moses. And we have blessings that forty years have made us forget."

"And Maggie, I also confessed my sins, and with what you've told me, i know together we can both get out of Egypt."

"Great!" said Maggie. "It seems like that priest did a good job."

"Sure did," added Rufus. "Sometimes we get stuck at the Red Sea and can't see the promise land on the other side."

Chapter Six

The Tree of Life

Justin Raber was twenty-seven years of ignorance. He was a mechanic and could change oil with the best of them. If you wanted your car serviced or detailed, Justin was your man. When Justin finished detailing your car, it looked like it had just come from the showroom. However, Justin didn't know much of nothing about anything else. Computers threw him for a loop. His forte was servicing and/or detailing a car. That was his niche in life, and he was good at it—tops. He never complained and never wanted anything more. Contentment is a wonderful thing, even if you're ignorant, and don't know any better. And Justin was ignorant, not dumb, just ignorant. He never advanced beyond comic books. Don't ask him to do a crossword puzzle; it'd frustrate the devil out of him. His reading level might reach the sixth grade and that's probably stretching it. He didn't go into the military as he couldn't pass the entrance exam, although he'd probably been great at serving the jeeps, hummers, and diesel engines. The new smart cell phones bothered him, so he remained with a flip phone.

The good Lord watches over his own and Providence had led Justin to cross the path of Billy Baucus—his mentor. Billy taught economics at the Polaris Technical School and Justin's grandparents had enrolled him in the school. The school promised that anyone who enrolled and completed the course would be guaranteed a job; the school would see to it. So, Justin was enrolled. That's how he learned to service vehicles, cook, and even write a check. You'd be surprised how many graduates from high school can't write a check. Those three things were essential to survival in our modern technological world, and Justin had learned all three at Polaris. True to their word, upon graduation the school landed Justin a job with Pope's Palmetto Repair Shop. Justin fit right in and Mr. Pope soon discovered that Justin was the best money he'd ever spent; everyone liked Justin and when he wasn't servicing a car he was cleaning the shop and taking meticulous care of the tools Pope's Palmetto Repair Shop gained a reputation as the cleanest shop in the Palmetto State. All due to Justin Raber. Most repair shops are filthy dirty with old parts everywhere. Mechanics don't throw away anything, "Might use it down the road," they say.

Even after graduation Billy kept in touch with Justin. He was not only Justin's mentor, but his friend. They ate breakfast daily at the local Egg & Grill Cafe, and Billy picked Justin up on Sundays and took him to the Main Street Methodist Church, where Billy taught Sunday School. It was a given that wherever Billy went Justin tagged along. They were good for each other as Billy had been married, however, five years after marriage, Billy's wife was killed in a car accident. Billy never remarried and took Justin under his wing. "All things work together for good to them who love God and are called according to his purpose," (Romans 8:28, NKJV).

CHAPTER SIX

On this day they went to Arnold's Barber Shop. Arnold's Barber Shop was in the south end of Harrisonburg Virginia. There was the typical Barber pole out front and a wooden Indian There were Cherokee Indians in the area and the sign on the door read: "Get Scalped Here!" Apparently, no Indians complained about it; besides, Arnold claimed to be seventy-five percent Cherokee. Billy got into the chair as Arnold cranked it up and said, "Usual today, Billy?"

"Usual," Billy said, "Getting a bit thin on top."

"What's new?" asked Billy. If anything was going on in town, Arnold knew about it. A barber shop was the local gossip corner. No secrets were left unturned in the barber shop.

"Nothing much," said Arnold. "Two guys escaped from the prison north of town."

"How'd that happen?" asked Billy. "I heard no one ever escaped from there."

"Apparently, they were both in the infirmary and needed to be transported to the hospital," said Arnold. "Along the way, somehow, they overpowered the EMT's and escaped in the transport van."

"Sounds like an inside job," said Billy.

"That's the word out on the street," said Arnold.

While sitting in the chair Billy noticed a large jar in front of the cash register. He could see the words: TREE OF LIFE DONATIONS—Lisa Martin.

"What's with the jar, Arnold?" asked Billy. Justin looked up from the magazine he was looking at. It was a two-year-old magazine with lots of pictures which appealed to Justin. The front page had a picture of the Tesla electric car on it.

"Lisa Martin has acute lymphocytic leukemia," said Arnold in response. "We've taking up money for her; she's only eleven."

"Tree of life donations, interesting name," said Billy.

"Well, as you know the Tree of Life was in the Garden of Eden, and after the fall Adam and Eve were driven from the garden, never to return, however, the Tree of Life reappears in the Revelation."

"True," agreed Billy. "Very metaphorical."

"What's metaphorical," asked Justin, looking up from his magazine.

"Good question," said Arnold. "Perhaps Billy can explain it better than me."

"What's metaphorical," asked Justin a second time looking at Billy in the barber's chair.

"It's a figure of speech, Justin," said Billy. "The Tree of Life in the Garden of Eden provided fruit whereby Adam and Eve could eat and live forever. Once they sinned, they were driven out of the garden and not allowed to return. In their newfound sinful state, they were not allowed to eat the fruit and live forever.

"Why?" asked Justin.

"Because after the fall, i.e., after they've eaten the forbidden fruit, suddenly they're unholy, sinful—whereas before they were holy which means they were perfect like angels," said Billy. Justin looked confused.

"Remember, Justin," continued Billy. "In Sunday school, I said Jesus died on the cross for us, well, the cross is a metaphor which is our tree of life."

"What's that got to do with Lisa and these donations?" asked Justin.

"These donations of money help pay for Lisa's treatments which are very expensive," said Billy. "The money in the jar acts like fruit from…"

"I got it," interrupted Justin. "The Tree of Life."

"Good," said Billy. Arnold tilted Billy's head as he trimmed around his ears.

CHAPTER SIX

"Very good," said Arnold as he finished up Billy's hair. "I'm glad you explained it and not me." Arnold shook off the hair from Billy's apron and motioned for Justin to get into the chair—"Next, Justin?"

About that time a man walked in with a mask on, and it wasn't a pandemic mask! He had a black pistol in his hand and said, "Okay, don't anyone move, give me the money from your cash register." The man was about six feet tall and a slight scar above his right eye which was exposed above his mask. He had snake tattoos on both arms. Arnold responded by opening the cash register, and as he did so he pushed the silent alarm which immediately notified the police station that a robbery was in progress at the barber shop. Sirens could be heard in the distance which frightened the burglar. He grabbed Justin who had risen to get into the chair, and pushed Arnold aside, taking the cash from the drawer, and grabbed the Tree of Life donation jar, then shoved Justin out the front door into a waiting car. And off they went.

"Where are we going?" asked Justin.

"Shut up," said the man with the snake tattoos. "Go," he yelled at the driver. "I think the barber hit the silent alarm." They sped out of town and ten miles out of town turned into a dirt road leading into the woods. He pulled over into a clump of trees next to a pond. He removed his mask and got out of the car.

"How much did we get?" asked the driver.

The one with the tattoos said, "Only about seventy-five bucks, but maybe more from the donation jar."

"That's the Tree of Life donations," said Justin.

"Shut up!" said the tattooed man, and he looked inside the jar.

"What are you gonna' do with him?" asked the driver.

"I don't know, shoot him, I suppose," said the tattooed man.

"Shoot him, are you crazy?" said the driver. "I got seven years looking at me for armed robbery and I don't want a murder charge! Why did you bring him anyway?"

"He's our hostage, besides, he can identify you—why'd you take off your mask?"

"Let's just dump him, and go," said the driver. "We didn't need a hostage, the police weren't there yet, now we got kidnapping added to the charge."

"So, we might as well shoot him," repeated the tattooed man.

Justin said: "You took the Tree of Life donations for eleven-year-old, Lisa. She has cancer."

"I told you to shut up!" he said as he hit Justin on the head. Blood ran down Justin's face.

"That's Lisa's Tree of Life," Justin repeated. "You're the guys who escaped from prison."

"I said shut up!" Get out of the car." The tattooed man pushed Justin out the door.

"Wait here," he said to the driver. He grabbed Justin by the arm and dragged him over to a clump of trees by the pond. The driver waited and heard, "Pop, Pop," with the pistol. The tattooed man returned waving his gun. "It's done, let's get out of here."

He dumped the monies into a sack and threw the Tree of Life jar out the window as they drove off.

"What'd the boy say?" asked the driver as they sped down the road.

"Kept mumbling something about the Tree of Life," said the tattooed man.

"The Tree of Life, what's that?"

"Don't rightly know, or care," said the tattooed man "It was written on the jar that I threw out the window."

CHAPTER SIX

"Now they'll get us littering," said the driver.

"Yeah, add to that—escape from prison, robbery, kidnapping, murder, so let's never get caught, or you'll never see the light of day again!" said the tattooed man.

"Wow, the day started off simple," said the driver, "Now we've taken a life!"

"Yeah," said the tattooed man. "This is a dark world, and it's getting darker all the time."

Both the driver, and the tattooed man, were totally unaware of the fact that two thousand years ago a man was nailed to a tree. That Tree of Life made it possible for even hardened sinners to find peace and freedom. Oblivious to that truth, they sped down the road into more darkness.

Chapter Seven

Finders Keepers. Losers Weepers

In the heart of the dense forest, where the sunlight struggled to pierce through the thick canopy, Chris and Abel embarked on their annual hunting trip. The crispy winter air filled their lungs as they trekked through the snow deeper into the wilderness, relishing the beauty of the tranquility that surrounded them.

Snow had fallen early this year—two weeks before Thanksgiving. As they ventured further, their keen eyes caught sight of something peculiar among the foliage—a wrecked Piper Cub.

"I don't remember any recent plane crashes," said Abel. "Right," said Chris. "That makes me think this was a secret night flight, or something similar, no doubt moving drugs, and they crashed." "And it wasn't reported," said Abel. "Look what's on the side of the plane—a flag of Mexico!"

Chris and Abel had been friends since the seventh grade. Chris was taller and muscular, had played football for the Valley High Rebels, whereas Abel was lesser in size but athletic and had excelled in tennis. Chris ran the local Outpost Sports Shop for camping, hunting, and fishing. Their motto was: "If we don't have it, you don't need it."

Abel was the opposite of Chris and was a bookkeeper for the downtown appliance store. Abel was a regular in church with his family, whereas Chris was a Christmas and Easter worshipper. and had no family since he'd been divorced twice with no children. They circled the plane, cautiously. The winter sun glistening off the shiny metal of the plane. Inside the wreckage, they discovered a satchel, zipped shut. Beside the satchel lay two lifeless bodies, both beginning to smell despite the cold air of the forest. Both dead men had guns, and the passenger still clutched the handle of the satchel, as if he were protecting it; almost afraid to lose it.

Chris' heart raced as he reached for the satchel, his fingers trembling as he pried the dead man's fingers off the heavy bundle. When he zipped open the satchel his eyes bulged as he gazed upon stacks of cash. Eight million dollars was what the paper read on top of the green stuff.

Abel exclaimed, "Look, Chris, there's more money here than in the First Federal Bank! " It was obvious, that of the two lifeless bodies, one was the pilot and the other passenger a designated guard or negotiator. They were either buying drugs or paying someone off for being a distributor. Silence enveloped the forest as Chris and Abel exchanged incredulous glances. The weight of their discovery pressed heavily upon them as they grappled with a moral dilemma that threatened to tear apart their lifelong friendship.

"We could clear all our debts, Abel," said Chris. His voice in the cold breeze was a whisper but laced with desperation; "We could finally be free from the burdens that have plagued us for years."

Abel's brow furrowed, torn between his sense of righteousness and the allure of financial freedom. "But what about the authorities? What if someone comes looking for this money? We could be implicated in something far bigger than we realize."

"No one's going to' come looking for this money," argued Chris. "It's been laying out here for how long? For months? No one even knew the plane was down. I'm telling you—it's tax-free drug money!"

"Well," said Abel. "You're probably right on that—it's tax-free money all right. But you can't tell me that the drug Cartel people aren't looking for their eight million bucks. You know, they've got to be checking their routes and trying to determine what happened?"

The time passed as they debated their options. Abel thought they should contact the authorities, but Chris insisted otherwise. He said, "You know what will happen? The police will come out to investigate, and take the eight million, and report a plane went down with two dead men—and no mention of the money!"

"I suppose you're right," agreed Abel.

"I know I'm right," said Chris. "Now here you are a God-fearing man, isn't this a gift, a blessing from God? We can be debt free."

Finally, as the sun dipped below the horizon, casting long shadows across the forest floor, they reached a resolution. "We'll keep the money," said Abel. "But we have to be smart, very careful about this. We can't go spending money like crazy. We need to hold tight with it, for say, three months at least, to see if anything comes out about it. If nothing after three months, then we're good to go."

"Four million each," said Chris. "I'm going to' buy a new truck!"

"No, listen to me, Chris," Abel insisted. "We cannot start spending. We've got to sit tight and wait. If nothing happens, then we can spend—but cautiously, so people aren't wondering how we suddenly became so wealthy."

CHAPTER SEVEN

"Isn't that something, Abel?" said Chris. "Here we are, out here in the woods hunting, and suddenly we hit the jackpot! It's like winning the lottery. I tell you, my old buddy—it's a gift from God."

"Or the devil," Abel added.

"Abel," said Chris. I'm cold and it's getting dark, let's divide the money—four million each, and get out of here."

"What about the bodies?" asked Abel. "Do we just leave them?"

"If we report them," said Chris. "Then we'll be interrogated; besides, look at them—they're frozen stiff. So, let's get our money and get out of here, before we're implicated, somehow."

"Yeah, I guess you're right. Especially if this is drug money, we don't want the Cartel tracking us down. Just sit tight and wait," cautioned Abel.

"Agreed," said Chris.

They divided the money—four million dollars each, and returned to Abel's pick-up truck, and drove back to Abel's house. "Wow," said Chris as they rode along. "We went hunting today as lower middle-class people, and now we're loaded—upper middle-class. Heck, Abel, we're rich!"

"Yeah, rich, but remember—do not spend anything for three months! And mum is the word!"

+ + +

A month went by, and Chris had a date with a blond waitress from the Lowcountry Cafe. As they sat at the bar, Chris, drinking heavy, began to talk. "You know, sweetheart, I'm a blessed man. Yes ma'am, a blessed man!" He repeated the phrase, slurring his words.

"Oh," she said. "Why are you so blessed, is it because you're with me, or what?" She smiled and drank her beer.

"Well," said Chris looking around in the bar. "I'm just better off than most of these goons in this bar."

"Oh, I didn't know you were so wealthy. And if you're so blessed, why does your old truck have over one-hundred-seventy thousand miles?"

"Listen, Sweetheart—I could trade that truck tomorrow for a brand-new truck, if I wanted." He gulped down some more beer.

"Sure, you could, but you won't, because you don't make that much money at the Outpost. In fact, if you're so blessed why don't you buy the Outpost?"

"Listen," said Chris. "I could buy the Outpost tomorrow, if I wanted. I could even buy this bar; why, Sweetheart," he said downing another beer. "I'm about the richest man in this bar!"

"Yeah," she chuckled. "I'll tell you what you are—you're drunk! So drunk, that you're hallucinating!"

"I'm not drunk, and I'm not hallucinating. "I'm rich—four million dollars rich!"

"Oh, my gosh!" She laughed. "Four million dollars, Chris, you can't even afford a lottery ticket. Driving to this bar your truck groaned like a woman in labor!"

"Listen," said Chris. "You think I'm poor. Well, you have got another think coming! I'll just go out tomorrow and buy me a brand-new Toyota truck—with cash! One with four doors and a sunroof and all the bells and whistles!"

"Sure, you will," she said rolling her eyes. "Where you going to get seventy-five thousand dollars—you going to rob First Federal Bank?"

"Okay, that's it. I've had enough. I know you think I'm drunk. Well, listen, tomorrow when I drive up to the Lowcountry Cafe, look out the window. I'll be in my new truck! and it'll be paid for—cash on the barrel head!"

CHAPTER SEVEN

Next day, Chris did exactly that. He went down to the Toyota dealer and plopped down seventy-five thousand dollars for a brand new red four-door Toyota truck with all the bells and whistles. Then he drove straight to the Lowcountry Cafe. Walked in, sat down by the window where everyone could see his new truck, including his Sweetheart waitress friend.

She walked over to take his order. He pointed out the window. "Do you see it? Do you see it? " He motioned for her to lean over, and whispered in her ear, "Give me steak and eggs, honey, I'm a rich man; if you want a good tip, make it snappy."

She was astonished. "How did you do that? That can't be your truck?"

"Oh, yes, it is,"—he whipped out the receipt and stuck it in her face. "See, I told you. Paid in full!"

It didn't take long for words to get around—Chris Mullens bought a brand-new truck, and paid cash! Gossip was fast in that town, faster than a speeding bullet. Faster than two shakes of a dog's hind leg. Not only that, word was out that Chris also bought the Outpost for two-hundred thousand dollars! The rumor was that some rich uncle left him a ton of money. Word got back to Abel, well you guessed it, Abel was fit to be tied. He jumped into his old truck and sped down the road to Chris' apartment.

He rolled out of his truck, banged on Chris' door, and glared at the shiny new truck setting in Chris' driveway. Chris slowly opened the door. Abel burst through the door, knocking Chris backwards; "Are you crazy? What did we agree on, now we're both in trouble."

"Calm down, clam down," said Chris. "No one's showed up, the money's good. No one knows how much money we each have." He emphasized the word each.

"You're crazy—what if someone from the Cartel shows up. and if they do, we're dead! The way you're spending money, people will wonder how you got it?"

"Let 'em wonder, Abel. I don't care. Let 'em think a rich Uncle died and left me some money. I don't care, I'm tired of being poor and sitting on this pile of cash. It's giving me hemorrhoids."

"Hemorrhoids! You'll wish you had hemorrhoids! If someone from the Cartel shows up, we're both going to have lead poisoning! Chris, I haven't even told my wife, now she's bound to ask me how you became so wealthy?"

"Just tell her," said Chris. "Tell her God has blessed me. That I'm one of his chosen."

"Chosen? Chris, you don't even go to church."

"I do so—I go Christmas and Easter."

Abel was fuming when he left Chris. He knew he was going to have to tell his wife Lib. When he got home Lib was in the kitchen putting away groceries. "Abel," she said. "You know what I heard in the grocery store? Chris has come into a lot of money. Did a relative die and leave him a pile of money?"

"No, honey," said Abel. "He doesn't have a rich Uncle. He doesn't have a pot to sit on—he had nothing until we went hunting." Lib stopped what she was doing, turned, and looked at Abel. "What do you mean, until we went hunting?"

"Sit down, Lib, and I'll tell you what happened." She sat down by the kitchen table and Abel sat across from her. He began: "You know when we went hunting, we went deep in the woods looking for deer; no deer, but we found this Piper Cub that was wrecked. Apparently, it'd crashed during that heavy snow storm the first of the year. Two guys were in the plane, both dead and frozen stiff."

CHAPTER SEVEN

"And you never said anything about it? You didn't even report it to the authorities?"

"No, because it looked like the plane was from Mexico."

"What does that have to do with it?" asked Lib.

"Well, you see, these guys had guns…"

"But you said they were dead."

"Yes, they were, but they also had money—drug money, we think." Abel paused.

"Money," interrupted Lib. "How much money?"

"Eight million dollars!"

"Eight million dollars! And you never told me?"

"Listen, Lib, here's the problem. If that money is drug money, as we think it is, the Cartel will come looking for it. And if Chris and I are implicated, well, it could get dangerous."

"Oh my gosh, Abel. And you never said anything about this, and didn't report it, and, well, does Chris have the money?"

"Yes, and no," said Abel.

"What do you mean, yes and no?" Lib looked puzzled.

"Well, we both do. We divided the money—four million dollars each and decided to sit on it to see if anyone shows up looking for it." Lib, almost fell off her seat. "You mean to tell me that you have four million dollars and Chris has four million dollars!"

"Yes."

"Holly Molly! —and you have four million dollars. Where is it, Abel?" She jumped off her seat. "So that's why Chris is spending money. I thought you said that you were sitting on it to see if anyone comes collecting?"

"We are, but apparently Chris got drunk and ran his mouth to his girlfriend and couldn't wait any longer."

"Where is the money, Abel? Show me the money!"

"Honey, it's in a satchel in the shed."

"In the shed—go get it. I want to see it, to feel it—now!"

"Okay, okay, calm down, just hold on." Abel left the kitchen and went out back to the shed and retrieved the satchel—four million dollars. He dumped it out on the kitchen table. Lib's eyes grew large as saucers, as she reached down and clutched the green backs—a pile of hundred-dollar bills. Four million dollars' worth!"

"Oh my, oh my," she said. "I've never seen so much money! When were you going to tell me?"

"I was going to' wait three months and then tell you. I didn't want you worrying about it or losing sleep over it."

"You've got to be kidding' me. I can 't believe that you walked around, knowing you had four million dollars."

"Well, we still don't know if anyone shows up from Mexico looking for this money. Chris, let the cat out of the bag! After all," said Abel, "the plane is still out there."

"Oh, that's another thing I wanted to tell you—I heard in the grocery store that some hunter had found a plane with two dead bodies."

"What? Quickly, turn on the TV, to the news," said Abel. They raced to the living room and Lib turned the TV on with the remote.

"Good evening, this is Rob Burns, with WKSV—TV from Beckley, West Virginia. A plane has been found deep in the forest with two dead men. One was obviously the pilot, but both men had guns, and the plane had markings of Mexico. It is believed they were delivering drugs and crashed in the snowstorm of some months ago. Both passengers were frozen stiff, due to the severe cold spell, and the only identification found was a cell phone, no drugs, or money—but two pistols. The local police are cooperating with the FBI and Homeland Security over the crash. We'll bring you more news as the information comes in."

CHAPTER SEVEN

+ + +

In short order, Chris' girlfriend was brought in for questioning. Since learning about the plane crash, she'd put two and two together, and called the authorities. Chris, her boyfriend, suddenly had a pile of money. Where'd he get it? The police wanted to know. Next thing you know, Chris was sitting at a small table in the police station waiting to be interrogated.

"So, you went hunting?" "Yes," said Chris.

"Were you hunting by yourself?" "No," said Chris.

"Who were you hunting with?"

"Abel Roberts," said Chris.

"Abel Roberts," repeated the interrogator. "And you found the plane, but didn't report it?"

"Right, and it was getting colder, so we left."

"And you didn't think it necessary to report two dead men in a crashed plane?"

"We debated it, but decided to leave it, as we didn't want to be implicated—since we saw the plane was from Mexico."

"Drugs—is that what you thought; this was all about, drugs?"

"Yeah," said Chris. "That's what we thought."

"Did you see or find any money?" asked the officer.

"No."

"Then how is it that suddenly you've come into a lot of money—buying a new truck and the Outpost store where you work?"

"I had a rich Uncle who left me an inheritance."

"Well, Chris, I can tell you this—that all can be checked out very easily, and if you're lying, you're in trouble. I think we'll bring in Abel and talk to him."

"Go ahead," said Chris. "Abel will tell you the same thing." Chris knew he was lying. He wasn't sure what would happen to him, once they discovered no rich Uncle, and he wasn't sure what Abel would be telling them, since Abel was a Christian and always telling the truth. For once in his life, he began to pray…but he wasn't sure why God would listen to him.

+ + +

There was a knocking on Abel's door. Lib answered. "Are you Mrs. Abel Roberts?" the man asked. There were two men standing in front of the door.

"Yes," she said. "Who wants to know?"

They pushed through the door shoving her backwards. "And where is your husband, Mrs. Roberts?"

"I'm right here," said Abel. "Who are you?"

"You found our plane? Where is the money?" Abel stood there, frozen, and unable to speak. Lib said, "Oh, my heavens, I'm calling the police."

"No, lady, you're not calling anyone. You people have something that belongs to us, and we aim to get it. Now, hand it over." He flashed a gun, and Lib fainted. Abel moved to help her, "No, leave her, she just fainted, that's all. Get the money and hand it over—all eight million dollars!"

"I don't have eight million dollars; I only have four million. Chris has the rest."

"And Chris has been spending our money and now he's in jail being interrogated. so, we're going to give you both twenty-four hours to come up with the money or else!"

CHAPTER SEVEN

"What do you mean, or else? Abel asked with trepidation. Lib was beginning to stir on the floor.

"Else means you will lose both thumbs and both big toes—to start with. We will advance to other body parts from there, now we're talking eight million dollars—all of it."

"I have the four million," said Abel. "Not the rest, Chris has that, and he's been spending it." They interrupted Abel. "Doesn't matter. This is your last warning, we'll take the four million right now, and in twenty-four hours you and Chris had better have the other four million." Lib was stirring now, and groaning. "Throw some water on that woman," the man said. They pushed open the door and left. Lib began to come to life again, just as the doorbell rang.

"Oh no, they've come back," Abel said. The doorbell rang again, and again. Then there was loud knocking on the door. Lib was sitting up now, but still on the floor. "Abel Roberts, a man shouted outside the door. "Open up, we're the FBI."

When Lib heard the words—"the FBI," she fainted again. Back to the same spot on the floor. It was getting to be a habit. Abel, not knowing whether to help his wife, or get the door—decided on the door, as Lib looked as if she were fast asleep. Two FBI agents entered the room, saw Lib on the floor and asked, "What happened to her? Did they hurt her?"

"Oh, no sir," they were here a moment ago and threatened us, and Lib fainted, and when you knocked, she re-fainted, if I can say it like that."

"Well, when she wakes up, tell her we've got good news."

"Good news is something I'd like to hear," said Abel.

"We saw the two goons leaving your house, and they were intercepted down the road. They're in custody now along with some others who were expecting the eight million. We've been after these guys for six months. We knew they were flying in drugs and money, but didn't know where, until you guys found the plane that crashed. Our undercover agent had marked the money and until it showed up—your friend began spending it—we were at a loss. "

"Anyway, to make a long story short, Abel, you and Chris are heroes for inadvertently assisting law enforcement in dismantling a dangerous criminal network. A network that is worth a hundred million dollars. But I do need you to turn in half of the unspent money for evidence." Lib had come to life again, and heard the words, "turn in the money." She sat up and uttered, "See, Abel, I told you in the beginning to report the money, now we're in trouble."

"Well, Mrs. Roberts, had he reported the money, we might not have found the criminals involved. By keeping the money and Chris spending like a drunken sailor, it brought the crooks out of the woodwork—a major bust for the FBI and Homeland Security."

"So, we're broke again," said Lib as she sat down, dejected. "But what about Chris? Will he be charged, or what?"

"More good news," said the agent. "You guys helped bust a major criminal network. There's a reward of ten million dollars on these guys! That's five million each, for you and your friend, Chris." Lib heard those words and fainted again, for the third time—on the same spot!

About the Author

Alvin Shifflett is a native of the Shenandoah Valley of Virginia. He holds a B.S. degree in Business Administration from Bridgewater College, Bridgewater, Va., and a Master of Divinity from Ashland Theological seminary in Ashland, Ohio. He earned a Doctor of Ministry degree from a consortium off seminaries in Ohio—including Ashland and Delaware United Methodist Seminary, Delaware, Ohio, and Lutheran Theological Seminary in Columbus, Ohio.

He has published seven books:

1. Blue Jeans Theology of James
2. The Beast of the East
3. Night Auditor
4. Back Porch Theology
5. The Blue Ice Patrol
6. I've fallen and need help up.
7. Low Country Biblical Almanac

He lives in Ridgeland, SC, and pastors two Independent Methodist Churches in Ridgeland and Tillman, SC. He has a daughter in Bluffton, SC., and a son in Manassas, Va.

www.ingramcontent.com/pod-product-compliance
Lightning Source LLC
LaVergne TN
LVHW041712060526
838201LV00043B/697